Spirits
Dark and Light

Supernatural Tales
from the Five Civilized Tribes

Tim Tingle

August House Publishers, Inc.
LITTLE ROCK

Published 2006 by August House Publishers, Inc.
P.O. Box 3223, Little Rock, Arkansas 72203
www.augusthouse.com

Printed in the United States of America

10 9 8 7 6 5 4 3 2 1   HB

LIBRARY OF CONGRESS CATALOGING-IN-PUBLICATION DATA

Tingle, Tim.
    Spirits dark and light : supernatural tales from the
five civilized tribes / Tim Tingle.
        p.   cm.
    ISBN-13: 978-0-87483-778-0 (alk. paper)
    ISBN-10: 0-87483-778-2 (alk. paper)
    1. Five Civilized Tribes—Folklore. 2. Tales—Oklahoma.
    I. Title.

E78.O45T56   2006
398.208997—dc22

                                    2006042709

The paper used in this publication meets the minimum require-
ments of the American National Standard for Information
Sciences—Permanence of Paper for Printed Library Materials,
ANSI Z39.48.

CONTENTS

Cherokee Stories

Choctaw Stories

Chickasaw Stories

Creek Stories

Seminole Stories

Cherokee Stories

Numbering more than 250,000 tribal members, today's Cherokees comprise the second largest Indian population in America. Forced to leave their homeland in North Carolina, Georgia, and Tennessee, approximately 17,000 Cherokee people embarked on the Trail of Tears in 1835. Roughly 13,000 survived the grueling trek to their new home in Indian Territory, present-day Oklahoma. Descendants of survivors of this journey belong to either the Cherokee Nation of Oklahoma, with their capital located in Tahlequah, or the United Keetoowah Band, also located in eastern Oklahoma.

Ancestors of the Eastern Band of Cherokees managed to stay behind, hidden deep in the Great Smoky Mountains of North Carolina. Three bands—located in Georgia, Alabama, and Missouri—are state-recognized, and several smaller non-recognized communities can be found throughout the United States, including Arkansas, Tennessee, Texas, and California.

Traditionally, the Cherokee place great spiritual power in the number seven. Even today members of the seven clans pray to the seven directions on seven ceremonial grounds in eastern Oklahoma. While Christianity is firmly embedded in the religious life of most Cherokees, the old ways are very much alive, incorporated in traditional stomp-dance ceremonies and songs. Many of the ancient beliefs and customs of the Cherokee are said to have originated with the Ahnikutani priests, a religious sect who survived for many years in secrecy at a small Missouri community, Panther Swamp. The priests, referred to as the ancient ones, were the spiritual guardians of the people and keepers of prophecy. The tradition of the Ahnikutani, as secret keepers of the sacred, continues today in traditional Cherokee ceremonies and rituals.

Differing from other Southeastern tribes, the Cherokees speak a language derived from the Iroquoian language family. Creation stories also have a unique flavor. The Cherokee world is located between the Upper and Lower Worlds, and communal balance must be maintained to keep the Cherokee's Middle World, our everyday world, intact. The spirit beings of the Upper World are represented by the birds, chiefly the Eagle. Soaring to great heights, eagles are associated with the creator and invoke great spiritual influence. As seen in the story "Eagle Slayer," the penalties for killing an eagle can be severe, and entire communities suffer when a single member violates tradition.

The Lower World is inhabited by snakes and other subterranean dwellers. Snakes—or ndädû in the Cherokee language—hold great power, and killing one snake is considered a grave and fatal offense by all snakes. Fear of snakes is even transferred to the dream world, where ghost snakes are thought to be just as dangerous as living ones. Anyone experiencing snakebite in a dream must seek medical treatment. In the Cherokee world, killers of snakes best beware, for snakes will seek vengeance. In "The Hunter and the Snake," an entire town is held in the fearful clutches of a powerful snake, twenty feet in length, until an outsider risks his life for the mere adventure of the hunt.

Many other spiritual and physical dangers inhabit the Cherokee natural world. Illness, death, and misfortune are attributed to the Anisgi'na, or evil spirits. Medicine to combat these evils is collected by Cherokee doctors and placed in powerful bundles. In the dark shadowland of Cherokee country, the inhabitants are ever wary of evil spirits, witches, and conjurers that haunt the woodlands. Lurking just out of sight are Raven Mockers and Spearfinger, moving through the smoky mountain mist, stalking careless Cherokees.

Knowledge and respect of the old ways are oftentimes the most powerful allies against evil, and contemporary Cherokees demonstrate daily this faith in tradition, as well as a strong will to survive the ravages that history has thrust upon them. A recent revival of the famed "Trail of Tears" drama, performed in an outdoor amphitheater in Tahlequah, Oklahoma, gives a stirring rendition of Cherokee pride.

The Immortal Ones

An old man named Tobaccoburner once lived with his wife and granddaughter at the foot of Bald Mountain. Wing, as they called the girl, was fourteen years old. Though her parents lived next door, everybody seemed happiest with Wing under her grandparents' tutelage.

The three kept a large and abundant garden. They hoed and fertilized and smiled as they did so. They ate heartily— sweet potatoes, squash, melons, berries, and beans of all types. Tobaccoburner raised hogs for meat and kept milk cows in the barn, along with two old plow mules, Longboy and Slofoot. Grandmother kept far too many chickens. Wing enjoyed slipping away at night, while everyone slept, and leaving eggs for their neighbors.

Creeping into a friend's front yard and tossing bits of bacon to dogs who knew her anyway, Wing would shape a nest of straw and fill it with as many fresh eggs as were needed for everyone in the family to have two for breakfast. Grandmother knew of this, of course, and oftentimes the following morning would ask Wing to clean the floor of her muddy footprints.

Grandmother knew other things as well, things no one else knew. She knew why Wing had trouble with her parents, why she argued and stomped and sometimes yelled at them. Grandmother was secretly proud of Wing for her spirited ways.

The trouble had a simple cause. Wing loved her grandfather. She loved him with a wise and deep affection unusual for one so young. Wing's mother saw Tobaccoburner as a dim-witted old man and treated him so, mocking him behind his back. Wing's father, son to Tobaccoburner, went along rather than fight.

This is how they lived until the Immortal Ones appeared.

———

A town nine miles distant was having an all-night dance, with fiddlers and singers coming from all over Cherokee country. Everyone in town was going to the dance, and Grandmother sewed a fine blue dress for Wing to wear. The afternoon of the dance Wing's mother came to visit.

"You can ride with us," she told her daughter.

"I want to go with my grandparents," said Wing. Her mother took her by the arm and stepped to the front porch.

"You mean Tobaccoburner is going?" she said in a hushed voice. "What does that old man think he's doing? He can barely drive a wagon. It's not safe with him. You're not telling me they are planning on going?"

Wing glared at her mother, but before she could speak Grandmother opened the door and said, "Wing, your grandfather is not feeling so well. Maybe you should go with your folks tonight. We gonna stay here, I'm thinking."

Wing saw the satisfied look on her mother's face.

"You have always told me I was too young to go to all-night dances," Wing said. "I guess you are right. I will stay with my grandparents. They can be helpless, you know."

———

An hour later the wagons pulled out of town, filled with talking people and rich foods. Tobaccoburner and the two people who loved him most were left behind. The first indication of trouble was the sound of braying coming from the barn, two hours after sunset.

"What you think that noise is?" Grandmother asked. Tobaccoburner, rifle in hand, was already on his way out the back door. He held the lamp aloft as he entered the barn. His keen senses caught the smell of fresh blood and the sound of heavy breathing coming from the stalls. Tobaccoburner paused, overcome with the feeling that he was not alone in the barn. He stepped slowly to Longboy's stall. The mule lay with his throat cut, his chest heaving as he panted away his final breaths. Tobaccoburner stroked his ears and said, "Gonna miss you, old boy. You a good mule."

Rising, he turned to Slofoot's stall and stood before it briefly, bowing his head in prayer before entering. Slofoot was already dead. His blood lay in a thickening dark puddle at the base of his neck. Tobaccoburner sat on the brittle hay and wrapped his arms around the neck of his oldest mule, lifting his head onto his lap.

Moving from stall to stall, Tobaccoburner said his good-byes to his animal companions. Once he heard the sound of quick feet running past the stall wherein he knelt, but he saw no reason to give chase. This night was darker than any he had known, and more death would come soon enough.

He moved quickly to the house, hung the lantern on the rusty nail of a nearby tree, and called out, "Stay on the porch. Don't go to the barn." Wing and Grandmother joined him on the porch. "Stay here, so they can see you," he whispered.

Slamming the back door as if he were entering the house, he double-backed and hid in the shadows of a clump of pecan trees, with a full view of the barn. In the slippery moonlight he saw five young men leave the barn and cross his eastern pasture, running in the direction of his son's home.

When he returned to the house, Grandmother was alone.

"Where is Wing?" he asked.

"She took off after you. I couldn't stop her." Tobacco-burner searched the barn, moving from stall to stall and weeping openly at the sight of his dead animals. Grandmother searched every room in the house.

"Granddaughter. Wing," she called.

When Tobaccoburner returned to the house he found a

stack of rifles and ammunition by the back door. He recognized several guns as belonging to his neighbor to the west.

"Grandmother," he said, opening the back door, "where did these guns and ammunition come from?"

"I don't know. Let's get them in the house. Did you find Wing?"

"No, she was not in the barn."

"I am here." Wing's soft voice floated from the shadows of a hickory tree at the rear of the house. In a moment she appeared in the circle of lamplight, dragging three rifles by the barrels and carrying a pouch of ammunition over her shoulder.

"Wing, what you did was dangerous," Tobaccoburner said. "Those men have killed our livestock. They all dead— mules, cows, all dead. They would kill you, too."

"I was careful."

"Careful and brave both," Grandmother said. "But no more sneaking off tonight, promise me."

"I promise."

"You promise what?"

"I promise no more sneaking off tonight."

"Or any night," Grandmother said, trying to look stern in spite of the deep pride she felt at her granddaughter's deeds. When Wing looked at her without replying, she said, "You are right. More than tonight is too much to ask of a young girl. Besides," she said over her shoulder, "we may not see another night."

Tobaccoburner crouched near a window in the front room, peering over the sill every few minutes as he loaded the rifles. Soon he saw several men carrying lanterns approach his son's house. He grabbed the ammunition pouch and as many rifles as he could carry and dashed out the door.

Approaching the house from the rear, he ran crouched over, unseen by the intruders. He quickly skirted the side of the house and knelt at the corner of the front porch. Five Shawano warriors entered the front gate, carrying torches. Twenty more Shawanos, fierce and threatening in the flickering torchlight, huddled near the fence. Not yet ready for the killing to begin, Tobaccoburner fired a warning shot over their heads.

The rifle blast exploded the soft hum of evening noises.

The warriors fell to the ground.

"Grandfather, we are with you." He turned to see Grandmother and Wing creeping through the shadows in his direction.

"Oh," he said. "You shouldn't be here."

"You can't kill them all by yourself," Grandmother said. "We brought more guns."

"Look!" Wing called out, pointing to a ball of flames sailing toward the house. The Shawano warriors were hurling the torches. One struck the front porch and another landed in the side yard, illuminating Tobaccoburner, Grandmother, and Wing.

"They want to see how many we are, how many warriors they are facing," said Tobaccoburner. In the quick flash of light from the torches, he saw the shadowy figures of a dozen Cherokee fighters, armed with tomahawks and bows and arrows, moving from the rear of the house. He recognized none of these new allies.

The Shawanos began taunting Tobaccoburner, unaware of this new army. "Fierce Cherokee warriors, Old Man and Two Women," someone called, and in the mocking laughter that followed Tobaccoburner rose to his feet.

"They will not leave laughing," he said, shouldering his rifle and taking aim at the voices.

Before he could fire, a deep voice from over his shoulder said, "We are here for you, my friends." Tobaccoburner turned to see a tall Cherokee warrior, motioning for his men to crowd behind Tobaccoburner and his family. When his men were assembled and ready for battle, he nodded to Tobaccoburner and said, "Fire when you are ready, Grandfather. We will follow your lead."

Tobaccoburner fired into the darkness and the Shawanos stood to charge. The Cherokee leader flung his tomahawk into the darkness. A moment later a cry came from the Shawanos.

"Ahhhh!"

A cascade of arrows burst forth as a dozen Cherokee warriors, led by Tobaccoburner, leapt to their feet and chased the fleeing Shawanos.

"I want to fight," said Wing.

"No, they will need us to take care of the wounded," said Grandmother. "We should be home. Your grandfather will look for us there. Bring the guns. We have our own work to do."

Lightning flashed overhead as the Cherokees, flinging tomahawks as they ran, chased the bewildered Shawanos across Tobaccoburner's pastureland. The sky continued to flash yellow. The Shawanos found refuge in a cluster of boulders at the foot of Bald Mountain. Tobaccoburner watched in amazement as the Cherokees pointed their arrows to the sky and launched a volley of flint-pointed missiles. The arrows sailed far beyond the crouching Shawanos. From high in the sky, they hovered, quivering like divining rods, before turning in mid-air and raining down upon their helpless targets.

"The Immortal Ones," Tobaccoburner whispered to himself, "have come to our defense."

Soon the mountainside was covered with the wounded and dying. The Cherokee leader, followed by Tobaccoburner, approached the Shawanos. Only four remained alive, seeking cover among their dead comrades.

"Leave your weapons and go," he said. "Take nothing from the fallen. Return to your homes and tell your people that the

Cherokees of these mountains are protected. You are never to return."

As the four rose and fled, he turned to Tobaccoburner and said, "We will camp on the mountain tonight. When you see our fires and hear our singing, know that we watch over you."

It was after midnight when Tobaccoburner dragged his weary feet across the damp grass of his back yard. The yellow light of a lantern filtered through the kitchen window and Grandmother sat on the top porch step, leaning against a support.

"Come to the barn," she said.

"I am too tired to bury my dead animals. Tomorrow. They will still be there in the morning."

"Come," she said. "You will not be too tired when you see."

Even before these two old Cherokees entered the barn, Tobaccoburner knew of the miracle he was about to behold. The tears flowed down his cheeks and he gripped Grandmother's hand tight.

"They are alive," he said.

"Yes," she nodded. "All the blood gone, like it never happened."

Tobaccoburner and Grandmother sat for almost an hour on a wooden bench at the rear of the barn. They sat without speaking, listening instead to the sound of neighing and sweet whinnying. A hundred feet away, from her place at the foot of the hickory tree, Wing watched the fires and heard the singing of The Immortal Ones on the side of Bald Mountain.

"I can't wait for my parents to return," she thought to herself. "I will tell them of the respect they showed him, The Immortal Ones, and how they followed my grandfather's lead."

The Raven Mockers

The trouble started when Thomas entered the house of strangers who were not at home. Though he was a young man, barely eighteen years old, he was certainly old enough to know better. But exhaustion from seven days of hunting—seven hard days with nothing to show for his efforts—clouded his judgment. Realizing he was too far from his village to make the trip before dark, he looked for a place to safely pass the night. As he approached a homestead not far from the trail, he recalled passing the cabin just two days earlier and seeing an old man and woman working in their garden.

The cabin was bordered on the east side by a small creek, filled by trickling waters from a nearby spring. A dozen sycamore trees grew along the creek's edge. Thomas knelt, cupped his hands, and tasted the icy cold spring water. Dappled light, filtering through the sycamore leaves, cast playful shadows on the cabin wall and the smell of a cedar fire drifted through the open front door. Thomas stepped to the door and spoke softly.

"Hello. I hope you don't mind a visitor. Hello."

His greeting was met with silence. In the pause before he spoke again, the air grew cool and Thomas was overcome with a sense of darkness, as if the house and trees were watching his every move. He was yet too young to heed the warnings of the spirit, otherwise he would have turned and fled.

"They can't be far," he said aloud, as if to prove his courage. "I'll curl up in my blanket and greet the old ones when they come home."

Thomas entered the cabin and settled himself in a corner

away from the fireplace. The floorboards creaked as he eased himself against the wall. He had barely tucked his blanket tight around his legs when he heard the whoosh of wings, followed by the call of a raven. Soon an old man entered the house and began to build a fire. A few minutes later he heard another raven's call.

"My wife is finally home," said the old man.

When a stoop-shouldered old woman shuffled through the doorway, Thomas knew his life was in grave danger. He pulled the blanket over his chin and peered at the couple from the darkness.

"I have entered the home of Raven Mockers," he whispered to himself.

———

Thomas knew of the Raven Mockers. He had heard his grandfather talk of them, of how they appeared wrinkled and old from carrying the lives of so many dying ones.

"They creep into homes of the sick, especially the older and weaker folks," his grandfather had said. "They steal the heart of the dying one."

"Why?" asked Thomas.

"They take it home and cook it. It is the source of their strength, this flesh of the dying. They add to their own lives as many more days as they have stolen from the sick one."

"How do they keep from being seen?" Thomas asked.

"They are witches, Grandson, terrible witches. They fly in the night with sparks crackling in the air around them. They arrive in a rush of wind, but they are invisible to the human eye. Only a powerful doctor can see them. If they are spotted, they will die seven days later."

"Why are they called Raven Mockers?"

"They make the sound of a diving raven when they fly," his grandfather said. "If you hear that sound, be very careful. They are smart and evil witches."

From his hiding place in the dark corner of the old man's house Thomas recalled this conversation.

———

"Look what I brought!" the old man said proudly, holding up a piece of heart-shaped flesh dripping with blood. Thomas crouched in the shadows.

"Well, at least you found something," the woman said. "Too many doctors where I went. Everybody crying, but nobody dying."

"Too bad," he said, "but this should make a good supper for us both."

The woman stirred the fire and the room soon blazed with light. Thomas knew it was only a matter of time before he was seen. He pulled the blanket over himself and pretended to be asleep. He heard the heart sizzling on the fire as the room filled with the aroma of cooking meat. For long moments he listened to the soft sound of gnawing and chewing.

When the old man and woman finished their meal, he expected a conversation to follow. No one spoke, till the woman finally asked, "Were you home long before I got here?"

The man said nothing.

"Not long enough to get a good look around?" she said, and Thomas knew her voice was closer than before.

"He must have come in 'fore I got here," said the old man, and Thomas realized they were standing over him. He snored lightly and rolled to the corner as if turning in his sleep.

"Hey!" the old man shouted, kicking Thomas in the leg as he spoke. "What are you doing here?"

"What, huh?" said Thomas, as if waking up suddenly. "Where am I? Oh, I am sorry. I hope I didn't scare you. I was so sleepy, I didn't find anybody home and I came in and fell asleep. I should be going." He stood slowly, avoiding the eyes of the Raven Mockers.

"No reason to leave now," said the old man. "If we had known you were here, you could have had supper with us."

He stared at Thomas as he spoke, to see the boy's reaction.

"I would have liked that," said Thomas. "I was not so lucky as you in my hunting. I mean, you must have caught something. I smell the cooked meat."

"Yes, I was more fortunate than you. You say you were sleeping? Did you hear our talking?"

"Oh no," Thomas lied, knowing his life was at stake. "I guess I fell sound asleep."

"Well, you seem a good boy," the old woman said. "I'll make you a place to sleep here." She spread a blanket on the floor as far from the door as possible. "It will be warmer here. You can have breakfast with us in the morning."

Thomas knew better than to protest. The old man and woman were closely studying his every gesture and expression.

"Thank you so much," he said. He soon made small snoring noises, keeping his eyes closed even when the old man leaned so close to him he could smell the bloody meat on the man's foul breath.

"I think he knows nothing," he heard the old man say to his wife as he climbed into bed.

———

The next morning Thomas rose before the sun. He had trembled in fear for most of the night, and he felt the soreness in his back and shoulders. When he heard no movement from the old man and woman's bed, he hoped he could leave quietly without their knowing of his departure. He stood, rolled his blanket quickly, and turned to the doorway.

There stood the Raven Mockers, waiting for him.

"Leaving without breakfast?" said the old man. "You think we are rude people and would send you away hungry?"

"Oh, no," said Thomas. "I did not want to trouble you."

The old woman left the room and began cooking corn mush on an outdoor fire. "Sit here, and we will wait," said the old man, pointing to a table and chair. Thomas sat down and felt the old man's eyes staring at him.

"My wife and I sometimes quarrel like last night," he said. "I hope you did not hear our quarreling."

"I was too sleepy to hear anything," replied Thomas. The old woman began to cry soft, muffled cries. In a short while she entered the room and filled three bowls with the mush.

When Thomas hesitated, the old man said, "You are our guest. Please, eat first." Thomas took a small spoonful of mush and swallowed it. He nodded in approval. The three ate in silence.

"I should be going," he finally said. He stood and quickly exited the cabin. Once outside, he walked as fast as he dared till the path took a sharp turn, then he sprinted with all of his speed.

Thomas was several days' journey from his village. He stopped neither to hunt nor fish, surviving on berries and sleeping less than three hours a night. On the evening of the third day he saw the familiar lights of his village. He hurried to his grandfather's house and told him of the Raven Mockers.

"You have seen them," his grandfather said. "You have spotted the Raven Mockers. They will die seven days after being seen."

"What about the heart I saw them eating? Can it give them life?"

"Your medicine is stronger, Grandson, or they would have killed you. You say the old woman was crying?"

"Yes," Thomas said.

"She knew your coming meant their deaths. But we must be certain. Call your father and your uncles. Tell them I need to speak to them." Soon the men of the village crowded into the grandfather's house and made plans to visit the Raven Mockers.

Four days later, Thomas led twenty strong men to a small knoll overlooking the cabin of the Raven Mockers. The spring had dried up, and the sycamore limbs were twisted and barren of leaves.

"They won't show themselves again, not till they are dead," his grandfather said. "Seven days should come sometime before morning. We will wait here."

No one slept that night. The wind whipped with a fury. During a brief moment of silence just before dawn, Thomas pulled down his blanket and saw sparks flying over the campsite. He felt the foul breath of the old man on his cheek and heard the old woman crying.

"Grandson!"

"Yes," said Thomas.

"Keep your eyes closed and your blanket tight around you. It is the last flight of the Raven Mockers before their death."

The old woman's cries grew louder. The stench of the old man's breath was so strong Thomas wanted to throw back his blanket and fill his lungs with fresh air. Finally, overcome with exhaustion, he drifted into sleep. An hour later the first light of day peered over the treetops to the east. The men rose warily, casting nervous glances at the cabin below.

"Let's have a look, Thomas, just you and me," his grandfather said.

They slowly descended the hill and approached the cabin.

"Can this be the place where I slept just seven nights ago?" Thomas asked. The wood was rotting, and spider webs and fallen birdnests covered the porch. The cabin appeared as though it had been unoccupied for years.

"I guess even the home of Raven Mockers lives on stolen

time," said his grandfather. With no hesitation, he entered the cabin. "There they are, Grandson. Don't touch anything."

Thomas looked around his grandfather's waist and saw the old man and woman on the floor, curled up by the fireplace. Their skin was a mass of wrinkles, and patches of white hair littered the floor around their heads. Staying behind his grandfather, Thomas neared the Raven Mockers. The old man's toothless mouth gaped open as if he had died gasping for breath.

"Now you have seen the death of the living dead," said his grandfather. "Best we set fire to this place."

Thomas's father and uncles broke brittle branches from a dead sycamore tree and piled them around the house. His grandfather handed him a flaming torch. "You earned the pleasure," he said. Thomas tossed the torch through the door and stepped back. Soon the cabin erupted in blue and yellow flames.

As the men topped the first hill on their way home, Thomas heard laughter coming from the cabin below. He looked back and saw a group of people stepping, almost dancing, among the burning remains of the cabin.

"Nothing worth seeing there," said his grandfather. "Let's get along toward home."

"Who are they?" he asked.

"Other witches. They've heard what happened, and they are celebrating. Everybody has enemies, Grandson. Less powerful witches are especially jealous. No need to worry about them unless they bother us. Let 'em play."

Thomas looked over his shoulder and saw six men and five women tossing the burning and charred bones of the Raven Mockers high in the air.

Spearfinger

Sami Bushyhead was four years old when she first saw the old woman. All alone, she had wandered almost a mile from her village. Stepping into a clearing at the foot of a mountain, Sami saw a tall granite rock looming a hundred feet directly in front of her. The rock was covered with soft green and brown fungus. As she stood staring at it, the rock seemed to move.

Before Sami knew what was happening, the woman was coming for her. She was the color of the rock, dark brown, and deep wrinkles sliced across her cheeks, sharp-cut like the stone. Her green dress and shawl hung loosely on her skinny frame. Her arms were outstretched, and her long fingers reached for the girl.

Sami turned and ran to the path leading to town. Over her shoulder she heard the old woman laugh and say, "Later, my little dear. I will see you later. When I am older still and you are fatter, we will meet again."

When Sami reached the path and saw her brothers returning from the day's hunt, she looked behind her just as the old woman lifted a long bony finger from beneath her shawl and pointed it in her direction. Everything about the woman seemed sharp—her chin, her thin fingers, even her laughter, which cut through the evening like the blade of an icicle. Sami never forgot the old woman, or the words she said.

"Later, my little dear. I will see you later. When I am older still and you are fatter, we will meet again."

———

Several times a year, the Bushyhead family made a two-day journey to a nearby town for trading. These neighboring Cherokees were known for their spearheads and tools, and the Bushyheads made fine baskets and beaded clothing.

When Sami was seven, she accompanied her mother and father on her first trading trip. As they entered the town, she noticed an elderly woman sitting in the shade of a cypress tree on the banks of a slow-flowing creek. Her skin seemed to blend with the color of the earth, and in the shifting shadows her wrinkles danced like jagged scars across her face. As Sami drew near, the old woman lifted her eyes and moved her lips in a menacing grin. *My little dear*, Sami thought she whispered.

Sami turned to her father and considered telling him what she remembered about the old woman, but she knew he would think she was acting like a child. *He'll leave me behind next time, if I am scared of the people we meet*, she thought.

Sami's mother sat on a log in the town square while her father spread a blanket on the ground in front of her. The Bushyheads unpacked their shirts, dresses, and baskets. They were soon surrounded by curious onlookers, who returned to their homes and reappeared with items to trade.

Sami leaned against a tree trunk and began daydreaming, when she heard a voice above her say, "There are strawberries growing by the creek." She looked up to see a young boy a few years older than she was. His face wore a friendly smile. "My name is Swimmer," he said. "I'll show you where they grow. Come on. Your parents won't mind."

Sami glanced at her mother, who nodded and said, "Just don't be gone long. Here," she said, handing Sami a basket, "bring some berries back when you've eaten your fill."

Soon Sami and her new friend Swimmer were eating strawberries and tossing stones into the rippling green waters.

As the afternoon lengthened, a cloud passed overhead and Sami felt a chill in the air. The sky darkened, and the breeze sang a deep song in the pine trees.

"I'll be back in a minute," Swimmer said. "My grandfather will be wondering where I am." He leapt over the creek and disappeared in the woods on the opposite bank.

As soon as he was gone, Sami heard movement behind her. She turned to see a tall young woman looming over her. Her smile was pleasant, and she reached to touch Sami's hair.

"Sweet berries, juicy sweet berries, yes, my dear?" said the woman.

Sami nodded and held a berry to the woman.

"Umm, thank you, my sweet girl," she said, biting the berry and wiping the juice from her lips with a long finger. "You have something, looks like a spider web, in your hair. Let me comb it out for you."

The young woman eased herself behind Sami and began to comb her hair, starting at the scalp and ending in long strokes where Sami's hair touched the ground. The woman hummed and stroked, rocking in a gentle rhythm. Sami rocked as well, till her eyes fell closed, her head slumped to her chest, and she drifted into a deep and gentle sleep.

The woman sang, soft as the breeze:

Stay with me,
You will arise and come with me,
Come with me, come with me.

As the woman sang, the breeze grew to a strong wind, and her voice was lost in the sound of it. Sami awakened with a start and recognized the voice, a sharp, older voice—not that of a young woman. The woman read the fear in Sami's eyes.

"Stay with me," she said. Her skin dried and cracked into

sharp, stony crevices. Sami tried to move away, but the woman gripped her hair and pulled her close.

"No!" Sami screamed, but the woman grabbed her by the shoulders.

"Remember me?" she said, laughing her sharp laughter. The wind blew so hard Sami could barely make out the words she was hearing. Tree branches snapped and whirled about her face.

"Mother!" she called. "Father, help me!"

"The sun is shining in town, no one will be looking for you," the woman said, blowing her cold breath on Sami's face. The pointing finger of her right hand grew ten inches in length, and the fingernail grew into a long, twisting blade. The old woman sang a new and terrible song.

> Liver, I eat, tasty liver, tasty meat.
> Liver I eat, young liver, sweet.

The old woman held the girl tight by the waist. She drew her long fingernail across the front of Sami's dress, tearing the cloth.

Suddenly she screamed and loosened her grip. Sami fell to the ground and looked up to see Swimmer on the opposite bank, leaning to pick up a stone. The old woman was holding her head with her bony hand. Blood poured through her fingers. Sami saw a large stone at her feet and knew Swimmer had thrown it.

"Let her go!" he shouted. "Run, Sami! Jump over the creek!" he said, throwing the second stone. Sami leapt to her feet and took three steps in the direction of the creek. She jumped from the creek bank, then felt herself lifting like a bird in flight.

As Swimmer watched with disbelieving eyes, the woman grew to be seven feet tall and her skin shone like dark granite. His second stone shattered as it struck the old woman's forehead. With her arms dangling like tree branches, she took one long stride and snatched Sami from the air.

Swimmer fled to his parent's home. He burst into the house and told his mother what he had seen.

"The old woman is a Spearfinger," his mother said. "She is a witch who lives by eating the livers of her victims. We must hurry, or the girl will die."

The entire town was soon aroused with news of a Spearfinger nearby. From their log on the town square, the Bushyheads watched as parents frantically sought their children, urging them to hurry home.

"What is happening?" Sami's father asked a neighboring merchant.

"A Spearfinger was spotted down by the creek," the man replied. "She took a little girl, an out-of-towner."

Hearing this, Sami's mother leapt to her feet. "Sami!" She began to cry. "Where is Sami?"

Swimmer's mother approached the square with a quick walk and a sad purpose. Her walk slowed as she neared Sami's mother. She took the other woman's hands in her own and looked into her eyes with deep sympathy before speaking.

"Sami has been taken by the Spearfinger," she said. Sami's mother howled and grieved till the men carried her into a house far from the creek, lest her cries warn the witch that she was known throughout the town.

Elders gathered in the square. "Bring Swimmer so we might hear the story from him," an elder woman asked. When Swimmer came, he repeated the story he had told his mother.

"Where did you last see her?" Sami's father asked. Swimmer pointed toward the creek, and after only a few minutes, realizing the girl's survival depended on speed, the elders agreed upon a plan.

"Swimmer," the woman said, "we need your help. You are afraid of nothing, we know that. But today you must be more than brave. You must be smart. Our plan can work. The Spearfinger will never suspect your strength. That will be her undoing."

Young men were sent to dig a pit and cover it with brush and earth. They buried dozens of upturned and sharpened spikes in the floor of the pit.

Armed with a bag of stones, Swimmer made his way to the creek. Crouching in a clump of elderberry bushes on the creek bank, he watched as the Spearfinger ran her fingernail down the back of Sami's neck and spine, leaving a thick trail of blood.

Swimmer flung a handful of stones and fled into the woods. Unharmed but angry at being watched, the Spearfinger brushed aside the stones with a wave of her forearm.

"You will die for that," she hissed, and the trees shook from the wind of her breath. She shoved Sami to the ground and crossed the creek with one long stride. Swimmer dove into the thick vines and bushes, thinking the Spearfinger would be slowed by her enormous size, but the old woman slashed the air in front of her, cutting a wide swath in the underbrush.

Swimmer felt the swish of her dagger finger just behind him. At the sound of her next earth-pounding step, he rolled to the ground as the Spearfinger sliced at his neck.

Distracted by the boy, she overlooked the disturbed earth and branches in front of her and stepped onto the trap. The earth gave way, and she fell forty feet onto the floor of pine spikes. A loud crunching sound shook the air, followed by a long silence.

"Help me. Please, help me."

The voice rose from the pit, cracked and thin.

"Please. I am dying." The Cherokees, men and women both, knelt and peered into the pit.

"Oh, please," the Spearfinger cried, but her voice soon

deepened and took on a mocking tone. "Help me, won't you? Lean closer. I am hungry."

The Spearfinger was solid stone. Her body had shattered the stakes, and she now scrambled to climb the steep wall. The Cherokees rained arrows and spears into the pit, but the Spearfinger swatted them away and flung brittle laughter at her tormentors.

"Liver's blood!" she cried. "I smell your liver's blood!"

From a clump of cedar bushes, Swimmer watched the terrifying scene unfolding before him. The Spearfinger was climbing out of the pit, digging her nail deep into the earth wall and inching her way to the top. Seeing their arrows bounce off the Spearfinger's stone skin, the townspeople began to retreat.

In a soft whisper of wind, Swimmer felt a bird land on his shoulder. He turned and saw a small chickadee.

"Tell your father to aim for her heart," the chickadee said. "It lies in the tip of her finger. She will die if an arrow pierces her heart."

Swimmer ran from the protection of the cedars and gripped his kneeling father by the shoulders.

"Shoot her in the heart," Swimmer said.

"Son, nothing can stop her. She is stone, solid stone."

"Not her fingertip. Her heart is in her finger. You can kill her if you shoot her there."

The Spearfinger was lifting herself out of the pit as the villagers screamed and fled.

"Look!" Swimmer shouted. He pointed to the Spearfinger, where the chickadee had landed on her long, bony finger. Swimmer's father hesitated and looked at his son.

"Trust me," Swimmer said. His father took a deep breath and set his lips. He selected a small arrow with a sharp, thin point and fixed the arrow to the bowstring. He then turned to the pit, and his eyes narrowed with the full focus of his intent.

The Spearfinger now stood on the edge of the pit. She cast her gaze across the waves of fleeing men and women. Her eyes stopped on two figures crouching fifty feet in front of her. Ignoring the pointed arrow, she lifted her bony finger behind her. In her stone-cruel mind she saw her finger slicing the air and severing the heads of the two who knelt before her.

In the split second as her hand began its downward flight, Swimmer's father released the arrow.

THONG!

The arrow struck the Spearfinger beneath the fingernail. Her eyes grew large as blood spouted from her finger.

In a slow and eerie return to balance, a dark veil was lifted. Colors returned to the earth and sky, sunset and evening colors. In the moment of highest brillance, the Spearfinger shrank to the size of a small, withered woman, a quivering black insect silhouetted on the rose-hued sun. Waving her arms for balance, she stumbled and toppled backwards into the pit.

In the unison of ritual, the Cherokees emerged from the green woods. Many women unknowingly shuffled and swayed. All leaned to look at the pit below.

Dark blood decorated the tips of a dozen spikes. Still breathing, the old woman hung in midair, suspended from the spikes twenty feet from the floor. No sound emerged, not a single twisting leaf rustled in her dying throat. Her mouth moved slowly, shaping her final words.

HELP ME.

Swimmer and his mother and father were soon joined by Sami and her parents. Then came the others. Hovering together with family members, clutching close, the Cherokees beheld the scene in the pit. A wave of sorrow swept over Sami's mother, and with its passing she spoke.

"Pity the wicked," she said. "They hear no music. They have no love."

The Hunter and the Snake

Rain Woman loved her son, Blue Stone, with a driving passion, a passion that wrapped itself around him like a cocoon. She sought ways to protect the boy from even the smallest pains that come with growing. Before he could walk, she sought advice from a medicine man daily, probing him with every question that came to her mind.

"I worry about snakes," she said. "How can I protect him from snakes?"

"Find a gray road lizard," he said, "the kind that puffs his throat as he sits in the sun. Catch the first lizard you see in the spring."

"Is there nothing we can do till spring? He will soon be walking," she said.

"You must wait till spring. Catch the lizard and carry him to the child. Hold the lizard between the child's fingers. Then scratch his legs downward, not too hard. Do that, and he will see no snakes all summer long."

"Even if he plays by the water? Even if he climbs over rotten logs in the woods?"

"No snakes, all summer long," said the medicine man. As Rain Woman turned to go, he whispered a simple warning, not for the world of talk, but for the air to carry to her as if it were her own thought.

"With every cure comes a risk. Go easy with your seeking."

––––

When spring came, Rain Woman came to the medicine man, saying, "I have found the lizard and done as you say."

"Good," said the medicine man. "He will be safe from snakes. Do you still have the lizard?"

"Yes," she said.

"Well, you must let him go soon, but since you still have it, there is another cure. How does he sleep?"

"He is a fitful sleeper. He keeps us awake sometimes most of the night. But I don't mind. He is my son."

"If you rub the lizard on his head and throat, he will sleep quietly. But you must be careful. He can fall asleep anywhere."

"He will be safe with me," she said. "He is my son."

———

As the years passed and Blue Stone grew to be a lean and handsome young boy, his mother's fears came to pass. A snake as thick as a log came to live on the mountain to the north of town. His body was twenty feet long, a foot around, and he devoured small forest animals, even deer. Called *Uksuhi* by the medicine man, he never warned his victims.

"You must promise me never to go near the north mountain," Rain Woman warned her son. "The slope is littered with bones, victims of Uksuhi. Being alert will not help you, not with this snake."

Her warning was true. Slithering quiet as the deep river, the serpent would encircle an animal beneath the leaves of the forest floor. Circling and circling with his powerful body, he would slowly tighten the loop. Whichever way the victim turned, he was trapped, as the snake squeezed the breath from the writhing captive till death came as a welcome release from the pain of crushed bones and empty lungs.

———

One day Blue Stone followed his dog to the base of the north mountain. Suddenly, his dog darted after a small fox, up the slope of the mountain. Blue Stone dashed after him, forgetting where he was.

That night Blue Stone did not return home. His mother cried and wailed. At daybreak, his father and uncles, accompanied by four hunting dogs, climbed the mountain in search of the boy. Halfway up the slope, one uncle pointed to a spot twenty feet from a large tree stump.

"Is that Blue Stone's dog?" he asked.

"Yes, that's him," said the father. The small dog was cowering and shaking. He neither wagged his tail nor gave any sign of recognizing his family.

Bones of every description surrounded the stump. Some were white as chalk; some were yellow and still clung to pieces of flesh. In a scattering of freshly disturbed leaves, Blue Stone's father found what looked like the boy's remains. His bones were strewn about as if flung from the bottom of a large hole at the base of the stump.

They gathered the bones into a bundle and carried them to the boy's mother. Without speaking, Rain Woman took the bundle to a spot by the fire and sat with her eyes open for three days, wrapped in a thick blanket of guilt.

"We will kill the snake," said the father. "Our son will be avenged. No other parents should suffer as we do."

"No," she said, speaking for the first time since learning of the boy's death. "I will not be a widow as well as a grieving mother. The snake gives no warning. Others would surely die in the hunt for him." Nothing the others said convinced Rain Woman that avenging her son's death was worth the risk to her husband.

"Is there no protection from the snake?" the people asked the medicine man.

"Uksuhi can be driven away by the smell of human sweat. But he is so quiet and lethal in his stalking. No on has a chance to run and bring on the sweat," he said. "It would be a foolish thing to try."

And so the town lived as under a cloud, bordered on the north by the snake, ever fearful that someday he would seek his victims in the town itself. Though the men spoke quietly of Blue Stone's death at family gatherings, they never spoke of it when Rain Woman was within earshot.

———

One day a traveling hunter walked into town. He was unfamiliar with the territory and sought advice from the boy's father.

"You can stay with us tonight and get on with your hunting tomorrow morning," the father said. "We'll be glad to outfit you with whatever supplies you need."

Tired from his long day's walk, the hunter accepted the offer. Other families came together for the evening meal, eager to hear tales of a distant land. The hunter proved to be a friendly and welcomed guest.

"Where I come from the woods are thick and the deer are plentiful," he said.

"The fishing," they asked. "How is the fishing?"

"Good fishing, also," came the reply.

"Then why leave such a place?" asked Rain Woman.

"I have heard of the mountains and the fantastic creatures to be found there," said the hunter. "I want to see these things while I am still young."

When he said this, the others looked down and said nothing. The brightness of the evening gave way as the boy's spirit cast a dark spell. Soon the hunter was bedded down and apparently sleeping in a corner of the grieving parents' home.

"We should have warned him," said Rain Woman.

"He is a hunter, strong enough to travel this distance," the father said. The uncles nodded, realizing the hunter was listening with aroused curiosity.

"I will tell him tomorrow to hunt anywhere but to the north," the father continued.

"Tell him why," Rain Woman insisted. The hunter lifted himself on his elbows, intent on catching every word.

"You are right, we can all tell him. But not tonight," said the father, taunting the hunter.

"No," said the uncles. "We can tell him tomorrow."

"Maybe he will not be discouraged at all," said the father. "When he hears of the murdering snake on the slope of the north mountain, he may be more interested than ever."

"He is smarter than that," Rain Woman said. "When he hears about how the snake crushes his victims . . ."

". . . and how huge he is," said one uncle.

"You are right," said the father. "He is too smart to go after that snake."

No! screamed the hunter, but only in his mind. *I am not that smart.*

"Who knows?" said the father. "Maybe this little hunter is not as young and inexperienced as he looks."

You will see who is young and inexperienced, thought the hunter. *Just wait till tomorrow.* He turned to the wall and began a long struggle with sleep.

———

Two hours before sunrise, the hunter was awakened by the sizzling sounds and smells of frying squirrel meat.

"Did you sleep well?" asked Rain Woman.

"Oh, yes, a fine and peaceful sleep," he replied.

"I have your breakfast. Before you go, my husband wants to talk to you."

After breakfast, the father gave the hunter a roll of dried meat. "Can I help you with anything else?" he asked.

"No. Thank you. You have been a good host to me."

"My wife wants me to warn you about hunting on the north mountain. It can be dangerous."

"I think I understand," said the hunter. "I heard talk of it—it must have been in a dream last night."

"You know of the snake, then?"

"Yes," the hunter said. "My steps go to the south."

When he departed, the hunter spoke the truth. His first one hundred steps pointed south. As soon as he was out of sight of the house, he turned north and hastily began his ascent of the mountain. From the shadows of a pine grove, the uncles watched the hunter and gave the news to the boy's father.

The hunter was halfway up the slope when he saw the leaves of the forest floor shake and move in a tightening circle around him. His heart pumped fast and his palms began to sweat as he saw the length of the monstrous serpent. When the circle was only five feet from him, the hunter leapt outside the loop and ran uphill with all his speed. The snake uncurled and soon caught the hunter as he topped the mountain. He looped his body around the hunter's chest and began to squeeze. The hunter was young and strong. He was also dripping with sweat from his run.

Remembering how snakes are repelled by human smells, the hunter ran his hands through his wet hair and across his chest and belly. He slipped his arm beneath the slick body of the reptile. Forcing the snake's head to face his own, he found himself staring into its death-dark eyes. The flickering tongue danced across his face.

Losing his struggle for life and breath, the hunter thrust his hands, dripping with sweat, into the snake's face. Hissing and gasping, flinging his head back and forth, suffocating in the cloud of human smells, the creature slowly uncurled. The hunter fell to the ground.

The hunter felt his side and winced at the throb of two broken ribs. Ignoring the pain, he rose to his feet and approached the writhing snake, without caution but with a sense of why he was sent to this town. He drew his knife and stabbed the dark reptile about the neck, over and over till the snake lay dead.

When the snake finished twitching and rolling his muscles, the hunter sat down amidst the carnage. His breath came in deep and painful gulps. Half an hour later, he stood and began his descent.

"The townsfolk will celebrate tonight," he said to himself. As he passed the tree stump, he saw movement from inside the pit. He paused in readiness and dread, never having considered the snake might have a mate.

The hunter was stunned to see a young boy climb out of the hole. The boy wore only a small animal skin and was covered with dirt and scratches.

"Did you kill the snake?" the boy asked.

"Yes," said the hunter. "He is dead. How did you get here?"

"I have lived here for too long, eating whatever he would bring me, raw animals, anything." The boy flung his arms around the hunter and sobbed. "Will you take me home?"

Soon Blue Stone was reunited with his family. Having twice been smothered, but still surviving, the boy reveled in a new strength, to the fierce pride of his father and Rain Woman, his mother.

Eagle Slayer

When the old men spoke, Panther listened with keen and eager ears. He was a tiny boy with big brown eyes, eyes that beamed when Grandfather looked his way. Of all the stories he heard, Panther liked those about the eagle the best.

"He is the most powerful of all creatures, stronger even than Man," Grandfather said one day, sitting with the children by the creek. When Grandfather lowered his voice and talked in hushed tones of the eagle slayer, the children held their breath and did not move.

"A man who lived in the mountains," said Grandfather, "was awakened one night by the sound of wind whirling about his hunting cabin. Earlier that day he had killed a deer. Looking out the window, he saw an eagle tearing apart the body of the deer as it hung on the drying pole.

"As a young boy, this hunter had heard the stories of those who ignored the proper ways to kill an eagle. He knew the tale of a man who deliberately killed an eagle in defiance of the respected ways. That man, they say, was tormented for years by eagle dreams, nightmares of birds attacking him from the sky, until he was cleansed."

Thus from his childhood Panther knew the proper handling of a slain eagle. He knew also the tragic stories of those who ignored the warnings.

———

One day Panther's beliefs were challenged. Now a strong young man, he went on his first hunting trip alone, staying in the cabin of a friend. He killed a fine buck and hung him to dry. As in the tale, Panther heard clawing sounds late that night and saw an eagle devouring his kill. Grabbing his bow and arrows, Panther ignored the stories. He saw only *this* eagle devouring *his* deer. His only thought was to protect his meat, his family's meat. He quickly ran outside and sent an arrow into the eagle's breast. The eagle fell over dead.

He dragged the deer inside the cabin to protect it from other predators and returned to sleep, leaving the eagle where it lay. Since the killing of the eagle was not a deliberate act of eagle hunting, he might have saved his people from the grief that was to come had he begun to respect the proper ways. The slain deer should be left as a sacrifice, and though Panther knew this, his first thought was to protect his deer meat.

The next morning he began the long trek to town, carrying the deer. He again left the eagle where it had fallen. Depositing the deer at his home for his family to attend to, Panther made his way to the home of the chief.

"I have killed an eagle," he said.

"Let us have an eagle dance," said the chief. "We can begin preparations now. The feathers will be useful." He called all together, and they began cleaning the eagle feather house.

"Should we get the eagle now?" asked Panther.

Cherokee medicine required that four days be given for small parasites to clean the eagle for proper handling before it was carried into the village.

"Yes, others may find the eagle," said the chief, "other animals as well. We will go now."

Cherokee men were sent to the mountain to retrieve the eagle. Rather than taking only the feathers and leaving the eagle's body on the ground where it was slain, as was the proper way, the men took the entire eagle. By afternoon, they carried the eagle's body down the mountain slope. The eagle was taken into the town and placed there for all to see.

That very night they began an eagle dance in the townhouse. Singing filled the night air, and seven elders played turtle-shell rattles. After midnight a stranger, dressed in a black shirt and britches, entered the townhouse. His hat was wide-brimmed, and he wore it low over his eyes, casting a shadow across his thin, bony face. His nose was long and thin, and no light shone from his eyes. The stranger gave a loud cry, silencing the singers, and stepped into the light of the circle, shaking his own rattle as he did so. Assuming he came from a neighboring town, they allowed him to speak.

"I have killed a man," he said, and told a lengthy story of a man who died for ignoring the right ways. Everyone leaned forward, drawn into the dark tale. At the close of the story, after a long silence, the stranger gave a loud and startling shout, shaking the rattle in a way that made the turtle cry. The listeners were stunned and fell backwards.

The silence that followed was brief, for with a weak shifting sound, a rattle held by one of the seven singers dropped to the ground. All eyes went to the singer, and all saw him fall over dead. The people were hypnotized with fear at the power of this newcomer. They sat unable to move as the stranger began another story.

"I have killed another," said the man. Again the listeners were wrapped with the magic of the story, only to be shocked at its conclusion by a cry that sent another of the seven elders to his death.

Dark terror gripped the townhouse. All who were present feared for their lives. Some struggled in an effort to stand, hoping to seize the stranger and drag him outside. Even these people discovered that their muscles would not move—they were frozen, forced to let the stranger have his way with them.

With the conclusion of each story came another loud shout as another elder dropped his rattle and fell over dead. When all seven lay slumped on the ground of the townhouse, the stranger ceased his singing and speaking. He left the gathering, and the townhouse swam with the smell of death.

Later, the people of this town called a trained and respectful eagle killer to cleanse their town of the eagle's vengeance.

"Who was the stranger?" they asked.

After following the songs and ways to ask forgiveness, he told them.

"He was the brother of the eagle killed by Panther."

———

Panther lived to have a family of his own, with many grandchildren. Whenever the evening sky streaked with sunset colors, his thoughts would often travel to the slain eagle and to the men of his hometown who died for his careless deed. As an old man, Panther knew the proper prayers, and after saying them, he would throw off his cloak of sadness and slowly walk to a stump on the edge of town. Young people followed.

"Children," he would begin. "Let me tell you of the eagle. He is more powerful than Man. One day a young man killed a deer, and that night he heard a noise. Looking out the window, he saw an eagle tearing apart the body of the deer as it hung on the drying pole."

In the children's eyes he saw understanding, and in the telling of the tale Panther lost his grief and soared with the strength of an eagle.

———

Choctaw Stories

The Choctaw Indians of today include two principal nations and other less populous groupings throughout the southern United States. The Choctaw Nation of Oklahoma is composed of 160,000 Choctaws whose ancestors survived the Trail of Tears. The Mississippi Choctaw Indians, located near Philadelphia, are descended from those who chose to remain in their homeland. As did those on the trail, they suffered unimaginable hardships and indignities. Several smaller groups exist in Alabama and Louisiana, including the Choctaws of Bayou Lacombe, whose stories were recorded by government ethnographer David Bushnell in the 1920s.

Choctaws are a people of rivers and low-lying wetlands, and a trip through Choctaw folklore is dark, damp, and dripping with eerie noises from the thick swamp foliage. Traditional stories warn against traveling alone in the swamp at night, and death and lunacy often await those who challenge this taboo, as in the stories "Naloosa Falaya" and "Hashok Okwa Huiga."

While rabbit is the tribal trickster, he cavorts on a lighter stage; the shape-shifting owl is his nightly counterpart. Even today, contemporary Choctaw people of all walks of life stop and give pause when an owl calls, replaying memories of frightful tales and actual deaths of kinfolks related to unusual sightings of this mysterious nightbird.

A quiet and suspicion-breeding controversy exists among today's Choctaws, as many see owls as mere messengers of death, while others believe the owl to be a bringer of death. Whatever the significance, the preponderance of owl references in Spirits Dark and Light reflects a common feeling of extreme caution regarding owls throughout the Five Civilized Nations.

Traditional Choctaw society also includes the presence of witches, who can work for good or bad. A witch is more likely to influence events to the design of an individual, rather than for the common good. The differing opinions regarding the witch in "The Lady Who Changed" typifies a traditional

Choctaw outlook. When the witch appears as a shape-shifting owl, she has clearly taken a turn to the dark side.

Medicine among Choctaws, and other southeastern tribal cultures, is more inclusive than in western European thinking, and involves an entire state of being: physical, emotional, and psychological. Seemingly unrelated events, from a western viewpoint, affect the well-being of a person. Choctaw alikchis are good doctors who strive to restore balance; by singing certain chants, or by smoking a person, place, or object with burning cedar, sage, or other herbs or barks. Often alikchis prescribe medicine to be ingested by the ailing one.

Family relationships are the house wherein Choctaws dwell. Thus, family conflicts in Choctaw stories are cataclysmic struggles, running deep as common blood. Father-son struggles, as in "No Name," and the rejection of a son by his mother, described in "Deerboy and the Speckled Doe," tear at the very fabric of the Choctaw world-view. Bones of departed family members are considered sacred, and great care is taken to assure their proper handling. Objects belonging to the dead are carefully removed from the home, and are often buried to accompany the owner to the afterlife.

In typical Choctaw fashion, these narratives reflect a basic optimism and belief that good will prevail. Acknowledging the existence of darkness, Choctaw supernatural stories nevertheless shine with a lightness of spirit, the spirit of survival.

Naloosa Falaya

Nowadays there aren't as many things living in the swamp like in the old days. There used to be all manner of creatures, sitting on cypress stumps, sliding up out of the green swamp water, sunning on a dark dirt bank.

You might see yellow knots on a floating backwater log. Better not reach for it, it might have teeth. Maybe it looks like a pile of leaves lying on the ground. Better not step on it, it might be have fangs. Maybe it seems like a bunch of moss hanging from a tree limb. Better not touch it, it might have claws.

All manner of creatures used to live in the bayous and swamps. That's a Choctaw word, bayou, and Choctaws are no strangers to the swamps, either. They know all about Naloosa Falaya, too, and all his children.

Naloosa himself had beady little eyes. From a long way off you might think him to be a man, an old man the way his skin was all shriveled up, looking like a peach drying in the sun. He was one ugly man, Naloosa Falaya. Nobody ever saw any Missus Falaya, but there must have been one somewhere, with all those children, twenty children at least for every Naloosa.

Here's what those children liked to do. They would reach inside themselves, inside their stomachs. They did this by digging and poking around about their navels. They would poke their own navels with sharp fingernails till they'd push and poke and pop right through. Then they'd grab their own entrails and commence to pulling. They would pull everything out, the large and small of it.

But they don't stop there. Some people say they'd tie their own guts to a tree and start running around that tree.

They'd keep on running till everything—all their insides, their lungs and livers and kidneys and all of it, all but the heart—was wrapped around that tree. After all this, the children of Naloosa Falaya were so light they would just float up off the ground. The slightest little breeze would come along and lift them right off the ground, like spirit people.

When morning broke through the trees, the sun shone right through them. They didn't cast a shadow even—none at all, not the children of Naloosa Falaya. When they finished with their night-prowling, they went back to the tree, poked a little piece of their gut into their navel, and went running around that tree going the opposite way till they were all filled up with themselves all over again.

Naloosa Falaya himself had no time for such foolishness. Oh, he could have done it, but he had no time for it. He was too busy working on people. In the old days, when a Choctaw hunter went too deep in the swamp, maybe he caught sight of Naloosa. Maybe he looked too long into those beady little eyes. Maybe he fell under the Naloosa man's spell. If he did, Naloosa might put a sticker burr, a witched-up sticker burr, on that Choctaw man. If Falaya man poked that sticker burr in the Choctaw man's skin, that man now had the power to do all manner of evil against anybody.

But the old people say the thing Naloosa Falaya liked to do best was to put that sticker burr on a Choctaw man's shirt. That way he'd carry the sticker burr home for his children to step on. When a little boy or little girl turned bad, sometimes it was the sticker-burr poison of Naloosa Falaya, like that little girl up on the Bayou Lacomb. It happened, they say, after the war with the Creeks, in the old days.

———

Redjack was the Choctaw, daddy of the girl. He got lost in the battle, lost in the dark of the deep night swamp.

Sometime in the night Redjack fell under the spell of Falaya man's eyes. Naloosa Falaya has powerful eyes. He poked a big spiny cocklebur through the skin of his thumb, got a little of his blood on it. The he pulled it out and stuck it on Redjack's shirttail.

There that cocklebur stayed till Redjack dragged himself home in about a week. Like it had eyes to see and a mind of his own, that cocklebur leapt off his shirt and right into a circle of children where they were playing on the ground. In a short while, the little girl stood up and stepped back. She felt the cocklebur drive deep in her heel.

"Ooooo!" She squalled and rolled in the dirt. She gritted her teeth and pulled the sticker burr out. But Naloosa Falaya had already worked his way under her skin. Mean old Falaya Man had found a way in.

The little Choctaw girl now did the strangest thing she ever did in her entire life. For all her future days she never did anything more strange than this. She took that sticker burr and turned around and poked it right back in her foot, right through the hard skin of her own foot. Then she stood up and mashed her heel down real good on it, feeling mean to the bone.

Meaner than mean, she didn't want anything to do with those other children. She ran off to the cornfield by herself, leaned up against a fresh young cornstalk, and when she felt it bend with her weight, the meanest little grin she ever grinned crept across that child's face. She reached around back behind herself and snapped that cornstalk. She felt so good and mean, shivers ran up and down her spin. Her eyes took on a beady look, and she knew right then and there what she would do that night while everybody slept.

All day long that little girl walked around in a deep river fog. That night, sometime in the wee hours, a little breeze blew through the window of her hut. She woke up feeling a light feather touch, soft on her cheek. When she opened her eyes, she couldn't believe what she saw.

Spirit children, dozens of spirit children, were floating all around the ceiling, in and out of the window, floating right through each other, all around her room. The children of Naloosa Falaya had come to play. They lifted her out of bed—it took six of them since she still had her inside entrails and all—and together they went flying through the window and over the cornfield.

It was some kind of witching party they had that night. The children of Naloosa Falaya and their young accomplice swooped down on the corn and started popping stalks like snap beans. But the meanest thing was yet to come. After destroying several acres of corn, they dug their fingers into the black mud, scooping up handfuls of soupy dirt. Then they carried it to wherever a Choctaw child lay sound and sleeping peaceful.

They threw it on their clothes. They wiped it in their hair. They daubed it on their noses. They flung it everywhere, making it look like the Choctaw children had been playing all night long and making mischief in the cornfield.

———

Before long, another bayou day came creeping up on that little Choctaw village. Before long seventeen Choctaw women, carrying baskets on their way to the cornfield, spotted the destruction and let fly wild howls of anger. The children heard the noise and wandered outside, sleepy-eyed and yawning. There they were for all the world to see. Four dozen Choctaw children and babies caked with mud.

All commotion ceased. Off in the bayou, the frogs stopped their croaking. The squirrels stopped their twittering. The snakes stopped their slithering. The magic was thick.

Old woman Estelline said it first, lifting her skinny arm

and slapping the air in front of her face, like she was waving old memories back to life.

"Falaya Man," she whispered. "Naloosa Falaya."

At the sound of that name, the whole village jumped to life. Every man and woman grabbed the nearest child and dragged those muddy bodies to the bathing hole by the river. They scrubbed the children good, looking for a sign. Finally, somebody hollered, "I found it! I found where Falaya Man left his mark."

They pulled the little Choctaw girl out of the water, held her down, and pulled the sticker burr out. The medicine man brought out his hollow horn and sucked the blood—and the poison of Naloosa Falaya—out of that girl. Everyone turned back to their work, and they had plenty to do, starting with corn planting.

Estelline warned them.

"Once Naloosa Falaya gets ahold of a child, he not likely to let loose so easy."

For the next many days, that girl's big brother followed her around, carrying his long-blade cane-cutting knife. One morning he trailed after her down to the river. He didn't notice it, but she was once again walking glazy-eyed, as in a fog. She sat on a big flat rock and started singing.

"Purty man. Come to me, purty man." When she reached out to something on the rock, her brother stood up to see what she was singing to. It was a big cottonmouth water moccasin, with his mouth wide open.

The brother pushed that poor girl aside and chopped off the head of the snake. While the snake lay there bleeding, his head rolled off the rock, plopped in the water, and sank slowly down to the bottom of the swamp.

Estelline said it was Naloosa Falaya, still trying to charm that girl.

———

Now I am not claiming this tale to have any moral attached to it. But if it did, it might be this: if you pull a sticker burr out of your foot, a hard sticker burr that hurts bad, once you get that sticker burr out, don't turn right around and poke it back in.

The Lady Who Changed

I never knew who she was. She lived as our neighbor to the west for as long as I can remember, in a small house through the dark oak woods. Even after the way she died, I never felt, like everybody else did, that I now knew her secret.

"She was only nice to git herself into our lives," they all said.

"Weaving her bad into us like rotten cane strips," said an old basket-maker.

I kept quiet, but I knew better. There were times when she was a nice lady. Once when I was fishing for crawdads in the creek, she brought me grapes—fat juicy grapes with big seeds, the spitting-out kind. Some people get mad and maybe sic their dogs on you if you get too close to their house, just wandering around hunting. This old woman would just wave and holler something friendly.

"If you catch anything, I get half!" The way she laughed while she said it, you knew she was joking.

Maybe part of her did not want to be what she was. Even after I lost part of my foot, I never blamed her. Maybe she was good, and the evil lived inside of her, like a hungry animal clawing away at her stomach from the inside. If I had not spotted her in the cornfield that afternoon, maybe it would have been different. Nobody likes to be hit upside the head with a stone.

———

My brother and I had spent all morning, from an hour before sunrise, digging a small trough in the ground, hoping to capture water from the creek that bordered our land to the west. We had seen no rain for at least six weeks.

"Work till the sun is overhead, then you can do some hunting if you like. But not till we get some water on those plants," my father had said. He rode to town, not to return till evening. We knew better than to sneak off without doing our work.

We finished the ditch and even dug several smaller troughs for the water to flow out onto the back acres of the corn patch. We were sleeping on the front porch after our noon meal, planning to do some squirrel hunting before nightfall. My brother woke me up as usual, talking in his sleep.

"*Go away!*" he shouted, kicking out with his boots. He could always turn over and go right back to sleep after a dream fight, but I was awake for good. I walked back to the cornfield to see how the thirsty plants were enjoying their drink. The ground was dark and damp all the way to the end of our trough, but no more water was flowing.

I was walking to the creek to see what the problem was when I saw her. At first I didn't know who she was. She wore a black dress I had never seen her wear. She was stooping over and rolling a stone into our ditch, building what looked like a small dam.

"Hey! What are you doing?" I shouted.

She turned, and I saw it was our neighbor.

"Oh," was all I could think of to say. It was strange to be fussing with her.

"You don't own the water," she said. She wouldn't look at me.

My shouts woke my brother up, and I could tell by the way he was running across the field that he would not talk about the problem as we were doing.

"You better leave," I told the woman.

"You better go back home," she said to me.

My brother could not have seen what she had done. He was too far away to see the dam. But I guess he could see that we were arguing. He picked up a stone and hurled it at her. I could hear the rock flying through the cornstalks. It struck her in the temple with an ugly *whap*.

She seemed to growl from deep in her throat. I stepped back, half-expecting her to turn into a dog and leap at me. Her hand went to her head, and blood spurted between her fingers. My brother was running at full speed toward us.

"You hurt her bad," I told him as he arrived in a huff. When I turned back to the woman, she was gone. Blood splatters covered the rock dam.

"Look," I said, pointing to the dam. "She was trying to keep us from drawing water from the creek."

"She doesn't own the creek," my brother said.

"She said we don't own the water," I told him.

"Well, she won't be saying that anymore," he replied. "We better move these rocks."

I had not noticed it before, but I now saw that my left boot was covered with blood. I sat down and removed the boot.

"You too lazy to help?" my brother said.

"Give me a minute. I gotta clean my boot."

"Dried blood never hurt anybody. Help me move these rocks."

Bootless, I stepped into the ditch and lifted a heavy stone. At first I thought a jagged piece of rock had shifted and dug into the side of my foot.

"Ouch!" I called out, leaning over to look at my foot. I heard a dry rattling sound—the sound that crawls under your skin and scares you to the heart. I moved to a slow stand, trying to spot the snake to know which way to go. I still did not know I had already been bitten.

I saw the diamond head of the snake in a patch of leaves

and dried grass at the edge of the ditch. Before I could lift my foot, he struck again. This time I felt the pain. I felt the rattler sink his fangs into my foot and shake his head to release every drop of venom. My brother pulled the snake from me and tossed it into the creek.

———

The next several days crawled by with my mind in a stupor. My whole body seemed to lump up in a hot ball of fever. My eyes were puffed up and I was blinded by the swelling. I lived in a dark dream of fleeing for my life and being caught, always being caught, by dogs with long pointed teeth. Smoke and songs and prayers tried to chase the dogs away, but they always caught me.

I later found out it was the fifth day when the largest dog of all finally caught me. His mouth was open wide, and as I lay helpless and unable to move he drew back his neck to strike. His teeth were shiny and silver as an axe blade. I remember this clearly.

The pain was so sharp I came out of my stupor. Half of my left foot now lay on the floor, flopping like a dying fish. My uncle held a small hatchet at his side. Seeing me awake, he dropped the hatchet and left the room.

My mother and my aunt lifted my leg and wrapped white rags around my foot, but the blood was flowing so fast it soaked the cloth dark red in a hurry.

"Get out the way, please," said my uncle. He had returned, carrying a small piece of smoking log. He pulled the cloth off and touched the burning end to my foot. My body jerked, and I was falling—away from my family, away from my home, screaming and falling and grabbing for something.

The lady who changed caught me. I landed in her arms and she held onto me.

"I am sorry. I didn't mean to hurt you," she said.

"Hoke," I told her.

When I woke up, it was dark and I was alone. I listened for any noises that would tell me what time it was. From the woods to the west I heard the call of an owl. That's how I knew this would not be over till somebody died.

———

Two weeks later, with everybody watching, I tried to stand up. It was no good. I leaned like a crippled horse. My uncle worked on my boot, stuffing a sock with cotton and wood chips. He poked it down my boot where the rest of my foot should be. Then he took a wood stake and carved it like a small crutch.

"Put your foot in," he told me. "Now stand up."

When I did, he tied the crutch to the side of my boot.

"You'll have to tie it every time you put your boot on from now on. But you oughtta be able to walk."

I tried real hard. I knew my uncle felt bad about cutting my foot. This would maybe make him feel better. I finally got the hang of it. I couldn't run, but I could at least walk *hoke*.

Shortly after I could walk again, we gathered the first corn. Mother made her corn soup, *pashofa*. It was thick and sweet. My brother and I roasted ears of corn over an outside fire.

Sometime after midnight, my brother started his dream fighting. He was yelling loud and throwing his fists. All of a sudden, he jumped from bed and ran out the back door. My father had to chase him through the cornfield and shake him awake, just to get him back to bed.

He was sick for three days before he could get up again. When he could get up, he got dressed and walked straight to the cornfield. He spent most of the morning pulling over stalks and crawling on his hands and knees, digging in the summer-hot dirt. He found what he was looking for.

At the end of the row we had harvested, he found a small doll that looked like a baby owl. It was made of cockleburs wrapped in tight cotton. Owl feathers were poked into the cotton to look like wings and a tail, and a broken piece of bark sat where the head should be.

"It was her," he said. "She buried this in the corn to make me sick."

The old folks, the singers and chanters, heard about the make-believe owl and began arriving that afternoon. They smoked cedar branches and shook the turtle-shell rattles. Early evening, they burned the doll in a small fire at the edge of the back yard while they sang old songs.

"She won't give up so easily," my brother said as he climbed into bed that night.

"What will she do?" I asked.

"She will wait till she thinks I'm not watching," he said.

"Then what?"

My brother gathered the covers and rolled over without speaking. For the first time since the rattlesnake, I was afraid—for my brother, for my family, for myself.

The next morning my brother spoke to my father in a quiet and serious voice. I couldn't hear what they said, but before they parted my father nodded and gripped my brother's shoulder to give him strength. My brother made a campsite beside the dam. He cleared a patch of ground of all plants—corn and weeds and grass—and scattered clean dirt in a wide circle. With his loaded shotgun, he sat in the center of the circle.

Mother had me bring him food. He just sat there, saying nothing. I stood and watched him from the cornrow, and when he thought I was gone, he started singing, singing and rocking. Just after supper, from my bedroom window, I saw my father carrying the clay moonshine jug out the back door.

"Where are you going with that?" my mother asked him.

"Taking it to the boy," my father said.

"He doesn't need that," she said.

"It's water. He wants her to think he's too weak to take care of himself."

"I hope you know what you are doing," said my mother. I could hear the worry in her voice. I was worried, too. I climbed out the bedroom window and stepped carefully through the cornstalks till I could get a good view of my brother's camp.

I saw him take the jug from my father. I saw him turn it up, hooking his finger through the loop on the neck and lifting the jug with his elbow, like the old men did. He took a big swig and wiped his lips.

Several swigs later, my brother leaned back and appeared to close his eyes. I was almost asleep myself, settling on my side, when I heard somebody approaching the camp through the cornfield. I sat up and waited for whoever it was to enter the clearing. My brother had not moved.

Suddenly, on the creek side of the clearing, I saw a large owl, an *opa*. She lifted her wings and began a gentle flapping motion. The hair on my brother's head moved with the breeze, but he kept his eyes closed. The owl scratched the dirt with her claws. She tilted her head as if studying my brother. Assured he was asleep, she lifted herself ten feet off the ground and began her descent. Her claws were pointed at my brother.

With a grace as swift as a deer's leap, my brother, my brave and smart big brother, shouldered his gun and sent feathers flying with a shotgun blast that shook the earth. When the dry dirt settled, he picked himself up from the gun's kick.

The owl was gone. My brother scrambled to his feet and pawed the ground with his fingers, looking for a sign. When the blood told him he had hit his mark, he sat down and shook all over. He wrapped his thick arms around himself, and I think I heard him crying.

———

The next morning, everyone gathered at our house again. My father and three other men walked over the creek and across our neighbor's back pasture. They found her lying a few feet from her house, dead from a gunshot wound. Since the snake had attacked me first, I was allowed to tag along and watch the burial. There were no prayers or singing or anything like usually happens when somebody dies. They just dug a hole and buried her not far from her house.

"Best to stay away from this place," my father told me. I nodded and took his hand to let him know I would keep my word. For the most part, I did. Except for that one time.

Come spring, the rains filled the creek to overflowing. No more crawdads for me; I was fishing for catfish. A log on the west side of the creek seemed to offer a good place to sit and lay my line in the water. I waded across the creek and settled on the log. I was baiting my hook when I noticed a small clump of grapevines growing around the west side of the log. They were the sweet purple grapes, the seed-spitting kind.

I filled my pockets with grapes. Once my line was in the water, I plopped myself on the ground, leaned back, and reached in my pocket for the grapes. I felt for and found a juicy fat one, placed it on my lips, and moved it around with my tongue. I was just about to bite into it, when something told me not to. Maybe it was a feeling; maybe the taste turned bitter. I only remember knowing that everything would change and I would have no control over it if I swallowed the grape.

I spit it out, emptied my pockets, pulled my fishing line out of the water, and hobbled my way home.

That was the last time I ever stepped on her land, west of the creek. Years later, when I would think about the old days and my brother, I would sometimes wonder—what would have happened, how would my life have been different, if I had swallowed the grape?

Hashok Okwa Huiga

There is a certain spirit that lives in marshy places, often along the edge of swamps. His name is Hashok Okwa Huiga and he is never seen during the day, only at night, and even then only his heart is visible. He appears in the form of a small ball of fire that moves over the swamp, just above the surface of the water. He moves slowly along marshy inlets, almost like a lantern looking for something.

Sometimes Hashok Okwa Huiga will hover in the center of the swamp and glow like noonday fire. If people approach, in the blink of an eye he can shrink to the size of a firefly. The Choctaw elders warn that if a person looks too long at the heart of Hashok Okwa Huiga, he will lose his destination and wander about in circles.

The warnings of the elders meant nothing to Jack John.

———

From ages long ago the Choctaws have always been hospitable people, especially generous to strangers. They are known to freely give food and lodging to help a traveler on his way. Even in their own village, a Choctaw family would never horde food but share it with those who had less. It is the old way, the way to be.

The old ways meant nothing to Jack John.

"People who live their lives following the tales of old men and women are hiding from the world," he was heard to say. When he was still a young man Jack John learned how easy it was to trick a traveler.

"You can tell a family from a far-off land just about anything and they'll believe you," he bragged to his friends. "You can tell them this berry is good to eat, or the water from that river is no good to drink. You can even tell them that if they don't leave a gift at the base of a certain tree, the people will be angry and try to harm them. Almost like a sacrifice to a god, they'll dig in their bags and leave their most valuable belongings under a tree in the woods. A tree in the woods! Then they treat you with so much respect, almost like you've done them a favor," he laughed. "People are fools."

His friends soon noticed Jack John's new clothing, made of cloth and decorated with beads no Choctaws had ever seen. He never told his friends the new trick he had learned, for even Jack John realized the danger posed by his latest venture. The first morning he decided to try it, Jack John stood on the main road a few miles from the Choctaw town and met a group of people passing through on their way to New Orleans.

"I can take you to a shortcut that will save you many miles," he told their leader.

"Is it dangerous, to be off the main road?" the man asked.

"Oh no. In fact, there has been talk of war between two local tribes. It will be much safer for you to stay out of sight," Jack John lied.

Against the advice of their own elders, who distrusted Jack John, these travelers followed him into the swamp. When night came he told them, "Be very quiet and do not build a fire. There may be warriors near."

When morning came their leader said, "We were told there were friendly people on the road. We are almost out of food. Can you help us?"

"I will be glad to help you," said Jack John. "I can bring you corn stew and hominy, if you have anything to trade."

The travelers were very poor. "We have nothing of real value," an old man said.

"Well, give what you can. I will return with the food in a few hours," he told them. The village was very close, but

Jack John delayed so long in returning, they thought he had traveled a great distance. He entered their campsite carrying leather pouches filled with fresh water and corn stew and bags of dried meat.

Spurred by their hunger, the travelers had made a pile of blankets for Jack John.

"Only blankets?" he asked, with a note of disappointment in his voice.

"And this. You can have this." He looked down to see a young boy holding aloft a fine hunting knife for him to take.

"It belonged to my grandfather. He stayed in the old country. You have saved our lives. My grandfather would be proud for you to have it," the boy said.

Jack John took the knife and held it up, watching the light dance on the sharp iron blade. He saw moisture in the boy's brown eyes.

"The blankets are enough," he said, handing the knife back. "You will need the knife where you are going." The boy smiled and nodded.

After their meal, Jack John led the people through a dark and snake-filled swamp, loading them three at a time on a boat he kept hidden there. When they disembarked two miles west of the Choctaw town, near the main road again, the people thanked Jack John, saying, "We hope you are passing through our new country someday and we can help you as you have helped us."

"I hope so, too," said Jack John, though being repaid for his deed would be quite a nightmare, as he well understood. Waving and smiling at the people as they left, he said to himself, "Those foolish travelers. It was too easy."

Jack John began stationing himself near the eastern entrance to the Choctaw town. Sometimes he did lead weary travelers to safe lodging and warm food. Although the elders suspected his motives, and indeed his friends understood fully his true intentions, he was allowed to linger on the road and greet strangers to the swamp country.

Soon he had many beautiful blankets and more clothing and weapons than he could ever use. As the months passed and his possessions grew, he realized he must find a hiding place. One night, wrapping his things into two colorful blankets, he eased himself into the darkness of the swamp, a darkness that was beginning to feel like home to Jack John.

Moving with confidence across the wet blackness, he spotted a small light at the base of a cypress tree. As he stared, unable to move his eyes away from the yellow pinpoint, the light grew brighter and brighter, till it cast long shadows deep into the swamp. Alligator eyes blinked on the surface of the water, and the moss hung like beautiful lace in the glare of the fireball.

Jack John's arms fell limp to his sides and everything—blankets, jewels, baskets, knives, and guns—fell to the ground. The light shrank to the size of a firefly and began to flit among the trees, darting in and out. Jack John followed it, wading through dangerous waters where unseen creatures lurked beneath the surface. For the remainder of the night Hashok Okwa Huiga danced and dazzled, luring his prey deeper into the swamp.

When daylight finally came, Jack John fell into a deep sleep. One arm flopped in the water and crawdads pinched him on the ears, but he slept through it all. When night came, Hashok Okwa Huiga, flaming bright, moved close enough to singe his eyebrows. Jack John awakened with a start.

Ignoring the nightcrawlers and insects clinging to his clothes, he moved to the light. Again and again, night after night, Jack John followed the swamplight, walking blindly through the mud and slime. He drank stale green water and grew so sick he could no longer walk—so he crawled. On hands and knees he crawled, never taking his eyes off the light.

Finally, he decided to end the madness. Knowing no other way, he clung to the trunk of a cypress tree, lifting himself to lean against it. He wrapped a thick vine around himself and waited for the alligators to find him. His wait was short. Two large yellow eyes soon came sliding through the water, eyes belonging to a sixteen-foot alligator. Powerful jaws opened and Jack John hung his head to the predator.

Suddenly, he felt himself falling. The vine rope loosened and he was dragged behind the tree. The alligator turned and swam away. When his mind cleared, Jack John looked into the face of a small boy with a big knife, a knife once belonging to his grandfather.

"We couldn't sleep last night," the boy said. "A strange light, like a giant firefly, kept us awake. We followed it here, to find you tied to a tree. What is happening?" Jack John saw faces of the travelers, smiling in joy at the rescue.

"Much has happened," said Jack John. "If you can take me home, I will tell you everything I remember."

———

Hashok Okwa Huiga still dances in the swamps, but Jack John never saw him again. In fact, till the day he died he never stepped foot in the swamp again. He lived out his life welcoming travelers into the warmth of his hometown, his good hometown, introducing them to the good people we call Choctaws.

Deerboy and the Speckled Doe

In the hills of Alabama once lived a Choctaw boy who longed to be a hunter. He became instead a deer. This is how it happened.

The boy was tall for a Choctaw, even when he was a child, and thinner than his older brothers. He had a quick mind and could outrun all except his oldest brother, both with his legs and with his thoughts.

"Father, will you take me hunting with you?" he asked one day when he was eight years old.

"You would just get in the way," his father told him. The boy's father was an older man and too impatient to teach an eager and energetic young one.

___

When the boy was fourteen years old and still had not had his guiding dream, he went into the woods alone, to fast and sleep and wait for his dream. Almost a week went by. The boy began to eat berries and finally caught a small fish to keep from starving. When he returned home without his dream, his father said, "Did you keep the fast? Did you think you would starve?"

"Yes," said the boy. "I was starving, so I ate only a few berries." He hesitated, then added, "And a fish, a small fish, but only after several days."

His father grew angry and told the boy, "Leave now, and do not come back without a dream."

"The boy is so thin now," said the boy's mother. "Leave him alone. He can go tomorrow. He will die in the woods. Look at him, he is so skinny."

The father gripped the boy by the arm and led him to the door.

"Go!" he said, pushing the boy outside.

The boy returned to the woods, determined to stay until he either died or had his guiding dream. After several days of fasting, he grew so weak that creatures from his delirious sleep slipped into his waking moments. One evening he arose, thinking for the final time, and with a strong will built a large fire. As dark crept through the woods, a beautiful Speckled Doe stepped into the firelight.

The boy quickly strung his bow and shot an arrow into the heart of the brown-eyed deer, fainting from the effort and falling to the ground as the arrow hit its mark. As he slept near the carcass of the Speckled Doe, he heard her crying, and her cries sounded almost human. When the boy awakened, the doe stood over him.

"Follow me," she said, bounding off into the woods.

He was so surprised to hear the doe speak that, without thinking, he arose and ran after her. The Speckled Doe led him deeper into the woods, where pine trees grew at strange angles, jutting through granite boulders on the rising mountain. Just as the boy thought he would topple over from exhaustion, the doe entered a large black cave. Aroused by curiosity, the boy followed. When his eyes adjusted to the darkness, he was standing before a majestic buck, the largest he had ever seen.

"My father," said the Speckled Doe, seeing the boy stare at the buck.

Scattered throughout the cave were piles of deer feet, antlers, and skins.

The buck motioned to the boy, nodding for him to approach and lie down before him, on the soft skin of a deer. The boy did as he was told, too tired to protest and uncertain if the entire trip to the mountain and into the cave were not an extraordinary vision. His doubts exploded in a sea of pain as the boy felt the deerskin pierce his skin and begin to grow into his arms and legs, shaping him like a deer.

A dozen deer surrounded him, fitting deer hooves to his feet and antlers to his head. The pain was more than the boy could bear. He opened his mouth to scream, but when he heard himself utter the thin cry of a deer, he fainted once more.

When he woke up, the skin clung to him, and when he stood up, he walked as a deer.

Back in the Choctaw village, the mother was grieving. During the boy's absence, his father had died a natural death, and when her son did not return from his vision dream, she was convinced he was now dead as well. When grieving period for her husband ended, the boy's mother led a group of singers into the woods, to the foot of the granite mountain, to sing the boy's death song.

From out of nowhere, it seemed, several deer came bounding toward them, led by a handsome young buck. With one powerful leap, the buck soared over the circle of singers and landed in the middle of them. The people were stunned. The chanters stopped their singing and sat very quiet as the buck moved about the circle, looking for the grieving mother.

When he stood before her, the mother recognized her son.

"Look at him!" she cried. "It is my son. He is alive."

"It is a deer," the lead singer said to her. "She is crazed with grief," he told the others.

The deer looked from the one to the other, as if he understood their words. Finally, he spoke. "Sing no death song for me," he said. "I have had my guiding vision. I am alive and very happy."

A frightened look crossed the face of the boy's mother.

"Catch him!" she shouted. Several men leapt upon the Deerboy and held him to the ground.

"Pull the deerhide from him," she said. "I want to see my son."

They tugged at the skin, gripping first the loose skin of his thighs.

"It is too tight. It is part of him," they said.

"Pull the deerskin from my son," the mother insisted. "He is still my son."

Again they tried to remove the skin, but when it tore and the Deerboy squealed and kicked his legs, they knew the skin was not merely covering the boy.

It *was* the boy.

"We cannot do it," they told her. "He is a deer. If we pull his skin away, he will die."

For long moments the mother said nothing. Finally, she hung her head and sighed. "I would rather bury my son," she said, "than see him live his life as a deer."

As they tore his skin away, Deerboy grew weaker and weaker. He stopped kicking and lay quietly. His chest heaved and his sporadic breathing sounded throughout the woods. The boy's eyes were covered with a thin gray veil, and the cloud of death hung heavy.

———

From a distant perch on the mountainside, Speckled Doe watched as the mourners closed in on Deerboy and seized him. She heard his death cry rise from the forest floor and saw his spirit lift to the mountain. Realizing she was about to lose him, the Speckled Doe ran faster than she had ever run in her life.

Soon, she was far above the treeline, leaping from boulder to boulder. As she reached the summit, she watched the spirit of Deerboy sail overhead. Speckled Doe took one tremendous leap and soared far over the edge of the mountain.

65

The next morning, Choctaw hunters found the body of the Speckled Doe, lying broken among the boulders at the base of the mountain. Her spirit was already far away, in the company of Deerboy.

The hunters brought the skin of the Speckled Doe to the mother of Deerboy, knowing it was an omen concerning her son. She sewed the two skins together to make a robe. On cold nights when she is lonely, she pulls the robe around herself. It is the cloak of her memories.

As for Deerboy and the Speckled Doe, they have much more than memories. In the land where the spirits dwell, they have each other.

No Name

Long ago, in the land of the Choctaws, lived a boy with a most unusual name. His name was No Name; for in the old way, you had to earn a name, by being especially cunning or brave, or slow and stupid, and you would be named accordingly. This was an old and important way.

No Name was neither swift nor slow, neither cunning nor stupid. He was so very average, he had No Name. You can imagine how his father liked this. One morning, when he was five years old, his father woke him and shook him, saying,

No Name, No Name,
Go hunting, go fishing, do something!
How can I be proud of a son
Who has No Name?

No Name leapt from his bed and ran behind his house to cry. He had planted a small oak tree, and as he leaned against his sapling tree it bent with his weight.

In town lived a girl named Whispering Wind, who moved as delicately as the breeze. She stepped so softly the dried leaves never crackled beneath her feet and no one ever knew she was there. When No Name was five, she was only four.

When Whispering Wind heard him crying, she slipped up behind him as he leaned against his tree. She moistened her lips with her tongue, then kissed him on the earlobe.

"Oh," he said, rubbing his wet ear. "Oh, it is you." Whispering Wind smiled her sweet child's smile and said,

No Name, No Name,
I will always love you,
Even though you have No Name.

"Well love me if you must, but leave me alone," he said, running into the woods to be alone. But when he thought of her, he said to himself, "She is a funny little girl," and happiness filled his heart.

When No Name was ten years old, his father was more impatient than ever. He woke him up one morning saying,

No Name, No Name,
Go hunting, go fishing, do something!
How can I be proud of a son
Who has No Name?

No Name ran outside to his tree. Its trunk was strong enough to support him now, and he leaned against the oak and cried, wrapping his arms around himself and hoping no one else had heard. Whispering Wind slipped up behind him, so quietly the yellowing sycamore leaves made no sound beneath her feet.

She moistened her lips and kissed him on the neck.

"Oh," he shouted, rubbing his neck and spinning around. "It is you! I should have known." Whispering Wind smiled and said to him,

No Name, No Name,
I will always love you,
Even though you have No Name.

"Well, love me if you must," he said, "but leave me alone." Whispering Wind looked after him, watching his every move as he walked into the woods to be alone. When he thought of her now, he said to himself, "She is becoming a beautiful young girl," and he smiled to think of her.

The age of twelve was a very important age for Choctaws in the old days. During the time of Green Corn, the young people would take part in a sacred ceremony to bring them into the adult tribe. A tribal elder, chosen for his wisdom, would take the young Choctaws, one at a time, into the river. When they stood chest deep in the water, he would wrap his arms around the shoulders of the young person and speak words meant for only that person to hear, path-wise words to follow for the remainder of their lives. The elder would then dip them full-body into the river.

As No Name eased himself into the river, the old man reached out to him, pulled him close, and said, "Be brave, and go into it." He placed his palm on the boy's forehead and dipped him backward into the river, squeezing his nose shut. The boy felt the water and the power of the words swirl around him as he wondered what they meant.

Stepping from the river, No Name was led to a place by the fire where he and the other twelve-year-olds were told the tribal stories to begin their understanding as adults. This was a sacred day of silence in the village.

It was well after midnight when No Name returned home. His father had kept the fire going and waited up to greet him. As he entered the house, his father stood and extended his open arms to his son.

"No Name," he said. "No Name. Today your father is proud." But when he heard himself say the word *proud*, something happened to his father. Long-buried feelings boiled inside him, and though he tried to stop them, he heard himself say words he would regret.

No Name, No Name.
Nothing has changed.

How can I be proud of a son
Who has No Name?

He put his hand on No Name's chest and shoved the boy, hard, sending him stumbling out the front door. Watching the look on his son's face, he tried with his hands to clutch the words and take them back, but words once uttered can never be taken back. No Name put his hands in front of his face and tried to block the words, but words can never be blocked by hands.

No Name, for the first time in his life, felt the pain of being an adult. He slowly closed the door on his father, circled the house with a heavy step, and slumped against his tree, sobbing.

She was waiting for him. She had heard. Everyone had heard. It was a thing of shame in the village. She touched the back of his neck and kissed him on the cheek, saying,

No Name, you know what I say is true.
I will always love you,
Even though you have No Name.

He turned to her and offered a brief smile. The tears flowed down her cheeks to see him hurting so.

"At least somebody does," he said. As he walked to the woods, she gripped his hand and took her place beside him for the first time. "At least somebody does," he said again, squeezing her hand.

———

The age of sixteen was an important age for Choctaw boys. If war was declared, boys of sixteen could join the warriors and fight. The young boys prayed for war, hoping to add new stories of their bravery to the tribal lore.

"We can earn new and better names," said the boys.

"And I can earn a name at all," No Name whispered quietly to himself.

The old people prayed for peace, for they knew that war brings with it Death. In this tragic story, the prayers of the young were answered.

Twenty Creek men camped far too close to the Choctaw village, and Choctaw scouts were sent out to discover their intentions. To their surprise, they saw the Creeks had no weapons, only tools for cutting. As the Choctaws watched, the Creek men began to cut, first small tree limbs, then small trees, and finally larger logs.

"They are cutting firewood. They are not hunting," they said to each other.

"They are not here to fight or make war, only for fire-wood," the scouts reported to the chief.

"They are too far from their homes to carry firewood," said the chief. "Watch them."

In the wee hours of the morning, while the Choctaws slept, the Creeks used the firewood as torches and began setting fires to the dried underbrush and cedar trees surrounding the town. The flames quickly climbed the parched trunks and leapt from tree to tree, creeping ever closer to the unsuspecting Choctaws. The Creeks then grabbed their tools and fled into the night woods. This was the worst insult one tribe could inflict on another, to burn a village down while the people slept.

Everyone was awakened and lines were formed, one from the river to the town and another from the river to the nearby woods. Men and women worked together, filling baskets with water and passing them back and forth to drown the fire. When the morning sun lifted itself over the horizon, it brought a tired and smoky dawn.

War was declared on the Creeks.

The young boys of sixteen years were taken from their families and given new weapons. They were taken to the woods and told the ways of the warrior. On the day the Choctaws were to leave their homes and fight the Creeks, the boys were taught a fire dance, a dance to make them strong in battle.

They circled the fire slowly at first, then faster, in hopes that the spirit of the fire would leap into the boys' hearts and they would become warriors. They moved to the sound of a vocable song, a song still sung today.

> *Way ho hannah hey yah,*
> *Heylo hey ya hey hey ya,*
> *Way ho hannah hey yah,*
> *Heylo hey ya hey heylo,*
>
> *Way! Ho! Hannah hey yah,*
> *Heylo hey ya hey hey ya,*
> *Hey! Ho! Way! Ho!*

The boys felt the power in the fire, and the spirit of the warrior entered their hearts. As they trailed after the Creeks, the path the men took wrapped itself behind No Name's house, where Whispering Wind stood by his red oak tree. He paused with his back to her, and she kissed him quickly and said,

> *No Name, bring back a brave name if you must.*
> *But come back to me,*
> *For I will always love you,*
> *Even though you have No Name.*

"I will bring back a braver name," he said, and she began to cry, knowing he had not heard her message.

The Creeks left a trail that was easy to follow.

"They are slow and stupid," said the young warriors. "Look how they walk, leaving tracks on the earth."

"They are cunning, these Creeks," said the elders. "This trail might be a trap."

The Creek trail skirted a large mountain and led far away

from the Choctaw hunting grounds, into territory unknown to this band of Choctaws. They came to a cave entrance tucked between boulders on the far side of the mountain.

"They have all entered the cave," said the young Choctaws. "There is no way out. We can slay them all."

"Be careful," said the elders. "It might be a trap."

On this tragic day, the warning words of the elders were ignored. Waving their weapons in the air, the young Choctaws entered the cave running. The elders were swept into the charge, some choosing to protect the young warriors, some simply caught in the onslaught.

They left only No Name to guard the cave.

There were no Creeks in the cave, but more than a hundred Creeks surrounded it, hiding among the boulders and pine trees. When the Choctaws were well inside the cave, the Creeks crept behind No Name and struck him in the back of the head with a large rock. Then they dragged an enormous gate from behind a boulder, a gate built to fit the mouth of the cave.

The gate was made of uprights of pine—dripping with resin, to burn quick and hot—and crossbars of green cypress wood, to burn smoky and slow. They lit the gate and watched as the flames crept and swirled around the pine, flashing and popping hot. When the flames met the cypress, the green wood sizzled. Dark, billowing clouds floated like smoky poison in the air.

The Choctaws saw the flames and ran to the entrance, but the fire covered the cave opening and they were flung back by the heat. They gathered at the rear of the cave, seeking pockets of air or another entrance. The Creeks waved the green smoke into the cave, and the Choctaws began to breathe the smoke and die.

Soon only one Choctaw, Bashpo Hattak, remained alive inside the cave. While others choked on the stifling air, he held his face close to the ground where the smoke did not settle. Seeing their enemy dead, the Creeks abandoned the mountainside, leaving No Name alive to tell the story.

When No Name awakened and saw the burning gate, he grabbed the crossbars with his hands and pulled and pulled, struggling with the heavy gate, but he could not move it. He removed his hands and caught the smell of his own simmering flesh. He did not look at his hands, knowing they would make him afraid.

The words of the old man in the river came to him: *"Be brave, and go into it."* He walked slowly to the gate, repeating the words: *"Be brave, and go into it."*

He stretched his arms through the gate, wrapped his arms around the crossbars, and lifted his legs. He rocked backwards with all of his weight till the gate began to rock, back and forth, and finally fell on top of him.

Rising from the floor in the cave, Bashpo saw the brave thing No Name had done. He ran to the gate and made a great effort to move it, brushing the flames aside with branches of a nearby tree, kicking at the crossbars, but the gate was strong and the fire burned with purpose.

When the flames lowered, Bashpo pried the gate with a large branch and lifted it from the dark and wrinkled figure of No Name, rasping his final breath.

In the old days, there were those who had the spirit touch, and Bashpo Hattak was one of them. He placed his two fingers on No Name's temples and lifted his face to the sky, calling out, *"Holitopama! Holitopama!"*

At the moment of his calling, Bashpo's spirit lifted into the Beyond, and No Name entered his body. It was a very strange thing, to be in the body of another. Some say for days and some say for months, No Name wandered in the shadows of forest and the wetness of the swamps, discovering who he was.

The people came from the Choctaw town and discovered

the bodies. Weeping family members carried the Choctaw warriors home. Hearing the cries of mourning, she came. Soft as a breeze came Whispering Wind. She accompanied the body of her No Name, walking behind his grandfather and mother.

When the Choctaws were placed upon the scaffolds to prepare them for burial, she lay in her bed for days without arising. Her mother and aunts brought her food, saying, "Eat and you will feel better."

"Take it away," she said. "I do not want to feel better."

"You must eat," they said.

"Place the food at the foot of the bed," she said, and when they did so, she kicked it to the floor. "Take it away, I told you."

She grew thinner and thinner every day. When they brought her a clay pot of water, she said, "Take it away."

"You must drink or you will die," they told her.

"Place it beside me and I will drink when I am ready." When they did so, she knocked the pot to the floor, breaking it. "Take it away now," she said.

No Name, knowing he would forever be inside this new body, returned to his town. He went to the home of Whispering Wind, telling no one who he was.

"I have come to see Whispering Wind," he said to her mother as he stood in the doorway. She looked curiously at him, and stepped aside, gesturing to her daughter.

No Name knelt beside her bed, saddened to see her sagging skin and protruding bones. "It is I, No Name," he said.

She opened her eyes with hope, but when she saw the face of another, she said, "You, go away."

When No name leaned over her, she put her hand in his chest and pushed him, hard. Surprised by the violence of her movements, he stumbled backwards. He was reminded of the night his father pushed him out of his home. His shoulders

slumped, as they did that night, and he felt a deep sob growing in his chest.

"How can I let her know who I am?" he asked himself. Then
he knew. The answer was in his chest, in the sobbing, in the
memory of how she had helped him, all those many times.

He slid beside her bed, lifted her head from the pillow
and softly turned it over. He moistened his lips and kissed her
on the back of the neck.

"Just like you would do for me," he said. "From the time
you were a little girl, you would kiss me on the ear and say
to me,

No Name, No Name,
I will always love you,
Even though you have No Name.

"I have come back for you. Come back to me."

He lifted her body from the bed and for a moment felt
her trembling like a bird in his arms. Then her eyes fluttered
and opened.

There he was before her, No Name.

His face was smiling, and his eyes shone to look at her.
Though he had the face of another, she knew that No Name
had come back for her. He took her to the river, and she began
to drink. That evening, she began to eat, and gradually her
strength returned. A week later, No Name and Whispering
Wind were married, telling no one who he was.

A month later, a naming ceremony was held for the one
who had returned.

A ceremonial fire was lit, and everyone in town came
together. The stories were told, and the families wept to hear
once more of how their loved ones died in the cave. When
the embers burned low and the time came for the one who
had returned to receive his name, No Name stood before the
elders, telling no one who he was.

"I would like to chose my own name," he said.

They wrinkled their brows and looked to one another.

"This is not done," said one. The elders huddled together and spoke. Though it was strange, they agreed, it was also unusual for only one man to return from battle. Maybe the spirits were at work.

"Yes," they decided. "You may choose your new name."

No Name stood by the fire and looked through the flames at the tear-streaked face of his father, who did not know who he was.

"I choose for myself a good name," he said. "I choose for myself a brave name. From this day forward, you may call me No Name."

His father lifted his face, and the tears dried on his copper cheeks. Pride filled his heart, and everyone in the Choctaw town felt this pride.

No Name and Whispering Wind lived a long and happy life, telling no one who he was. Well into his nineties, he finally died. After the proper bone-bundling of his body and the burial in the family mound, she knelt over his grave. She dug a handful of dirt from the dark earth and spread it over the mound. She moistened her lips and kissed the ground beneath which he lay, saying,

You see, No Name, it is just as I always promised.
I will always love you,
Even though you have No Name.

Chickasaw Stories

The Chickasaws originally occupied land in the rugged hill country of northeast Mississippi. Following the signing of the Doaksville Treaty in 1837, they were removed to Indian Territory, leasing land from the Choctaws and settling in what is today south-central Oklahoma. Better organized and with sufficient money to help them on their journey, the Chickasaws fared better than other travelers on the Trail of Tears.

Early legends link the Chickasaws with the Choctaws, and both peoples speak similar languages in the Muskogean family. An early migration story describes a journey from a land to the west by two brothers, Chahtah and Chikasah. Guided by a white dog, the travelers encamped each evening after planting a long pole in the ground. At daybreak, they would continue traveling in the direction the pole was leaning. When the pole was placed in a mound of dirt near present-day Philadelphia, Mississippi, the pole stood upright, and in some accounts dramatically dug itself deeper into the earth.

The followers of Chikasah crossed a small creek and set up camp. During the night severe flooding turned the stream into a rampaging river, and the two peoples were separated. Those following Chahtah remained near the earthen mound, Nanih Waiya, the Choctaw sacred mother mound, while followers of Chikasah continued north to settle.

Though legends and linguistic similarities suggest a common ancestry, the Chickasaws and Choctaws have at times fought like bitter siblings. The Chickasaws have, from the 1700s to the present, prided themselves as fierce combatants, and historical accounts give credence to this claim. While the Choctaws generally allied themselves with the French, the Chickasaws formed alliances with the British. In times of war, the Chickasaws took refuge in large towns surrounded by impenetrable barricades. In 1736, in a battle over control of the Mississippi River trade routes, Chickasaw warriors dealt the French their most severe beating ever in battle against American Indians.

During the Civil War, fighting on the side of the Confederacy, the Chickasaw Nation suffered greatly. In October of 1864, when Union cavalry raided the Chickasaw Nation, the loss of human life and homes was staggering. On August 5th, 1865, the Chickasaw Nation became the last political unit of the Confederacy to capitulate, months after Lee had surrendered at Appomattox.

At present the Chickasaw have only 300 acres that are tribally owned, but Chickasaw influence in central Oklahoma is strong. Federally recognized with an enrollment of more than 35,000, the Chickasaws are currently the eighth-largest tribe in the United States. As is the case with each of the Five Civilized Nations, the Chickasaws enjoy the benefits of modern comforts while they exhibit great pride in celebrating tribal culture.

A traditional Chickasaw diet consists of a variety of corn dishes, supplemented with deer and squirrels, and later beef and pork. Fear of the owl, or at least a healthy caution, is ever-present in Chickasaw thinking. Spiritual stories of the past one hundred years are replete with examples of returning from the dead. Oftentimes these visitations are friendly and bring closure to unfinished worldly events; other times a ghost is merely offering advice to the living, as in the stories "Emma's Mother," and "Back from the Grave."

The tragic story of innocence lost, "Rabbit Death," contains a warning of killing for pleasure and greed, expressing a strong Chickasaw belief. "Tracks in the Mud" is kin to many stories of Plains Indians, but the accompanying cultural elements are decidedly Chickasaw. This story in particular hints at the subtle cultural differences between those whose power hinges on money and those who depend on strong family ties. In the shifting world of Indian medicine, money holds little sway.

The Chickasaw Nation has recently embarked on a project to record stories and renew interest in the language. Undoubtedly, future generations of Chickasaws will be better able to retain their identity as a distinct and powerful force in Oklahoma.

Emma's Mother

Emma Anatubby lived in the shadow of her mother. The elder Anatubby woman was strong in her beliefs but quiet in sharing them—qualities that gave her high standing in the Chickasaw town they called home. Emma's father was a hardworking man content to let his wife make most decisions. She, in her turn, never corrected him or spoke against him in any way. She was as good as she was strong.

"Emma will have no problem in selecting a good husband," the women often said, seeing Emma grow into the beauty her mother once had been. "Her mother will see to that." Their predictions would come true, though in a way they would never have guessed.

Emma was approaching the age when young men looked down when she walked their way, and cast longing looks at her as she passed. In that regard, the timing of her mother's death could not have been more unfortunate. They found her on the back porch, slumped over in her rocking chair and looking to the western woods. She had no look of illness or struggle about her. She died a peaceful death, but her leaving cut into the heart of her husband.

"He will grieve until he dies," the family said, seeing the man's sagging posture and empty gaze.

Emma woke up every morning and lay in bed trying to remember what was wrong, what was that sting the night had taken from her. Every morning began with a soft and secret cry.

One morning, several weeks after her mother's death, Emma found herself walking in those western woods behind her house. She spotted a clump of blue flowers on a moist spot of ground and stooped to top pick them, as her friends would often do. She held a small bouquet and was looking for another color, maybe yellow, to carry home and place upon the table, before she realized she had never in her life picked flowers without her mother's permission. She would pick a blossom and carry it to her mother to know the meaning of this flower, the uses, the rightness or wrongness of picking it.

She missed her mother, but she loved the flowers, too.

————

As Emma sat that evening and looked to the woods, a man appeared. He walked with a tired step, as if he had traveled a great distance. He was older than Emma, ten years at least. Emma stood and watched as he neared, expecting him to see her, tip his hat, and veer away, passing her house on the way to the road. Instead, he came closer and closer, never looking up until he stood before her, standing a foot taller and a shade darker than Emma.

"If your father is here, I would like to speak to him," the stranger said. Without taking her eyes off the man, Emma called her father. As the two spoke, she stepped into the house and watched through the thin curtains of the kitchen.

"Who is he?" she asked when her father returned.

"He's looking for work. We need the help. He'll sleep in the barn."

————

As simple as that, the love of her life walked into Emma's world. He was, of course, as hardworking as her father had been in his younger days, with twice the strength. Emma cooked him three meals a day, always leaving the food on a barrel outside the barn, where the dogs couldn't get to it. Even before the townspeople set about their gossiping, the man, Ethan, asked permission from Emma's father to begin courting her.

One morning, after her second trip to the creek with

Ethan, Emma realized that she had ceased her crying. Before rising and beginning the day's work, she visited her mother's room.

"You know how much I miss you," she said, touching her mother's dresses and running her fingers over her mother's beads. "I need you so, to help me know if this is right."

That evening, Ethan asked her father for her hand in marriage.

"I would be proud to call you son," her father said. He knew his days were numbered and had prayed that Emma would be married before he died.

When the townspeople heard, true friends of the family were filled with joy, knowing how the old man longed for it.

Others, and there were many, said, "So soon after her mother died? And who is this man?"

"Where does he come from?" said some.

"Where is his family?" said others.

Even, "What is he running from?"

Ethan knew of their suspicions. How could it be otherwise? He began to accompany the old man to town, to help him lift and carry his purchases, to sit on the fringe of the old men's talking circles, waiting sometimes for hours without saying a word.

One day, Ethan leaned against a tree and pulled his hat over his face till the men thought he was sleeping. They quietly turned the conversation to the stranger set to marry sweet Emma.

"How is he at fishing?"

"I've never seen him fish," said Emma's father. The old men looked at one another, saying nothing.

The next morning, Emma's father said to Ethan, "How about you and I do some fishing at the creek?"

Emma smiled to hear this. The men in her life, she knew, must get along.

This day that started with such hope would end in darkest tragedy.

—

Emma sat in the early evening looking to the western woods, watching the sky streak with orange and yellow, seeing the fire of her heart painted on the sky.

"Emma!" Ethan called. "Emma! Please, Emma!" His cries seemed to be coming from deep in the woods.

Emma stood and waited. Time passed, far too long. She stumbled down the porch steps, clutching her dress as she ran into the thicket. Once in the dark of the woods, she felt suddenly afraid. Turning back to the house, she spotted Ethan fifty feet to her left, emerging from the woods and carrying something heavy in his arms.

"Did you catch a deer?" she asked, but the tears streaming down his face told her she was seeing something she wanted never to see. Her father—her elderly, small and good father—was dead, carried by the man she had promised to marry.

Ethan dragged his feet the final distance to the house and fell over the old man, crying from deep inside himself.

"He felt so young," he said. "He jumped from the boulders like a boy, happy to be fishing again. He was too old to act so young. He slipped and fell. I tried to catch him, but I was so slow. My arms moved so slow. I watched him fall. I could do nothing."

Emma knelt beside them both and wrapped her thin arms around the two men she loved. An hour later, when she rose, she thought of what her mother would do. She lifted Ethan to his feet and helped him carry the old man to the house. The two bathed and cleaned and stayed with him all night.

"My father died yesterday," she told the neighbors the next morning. "He fell and struck his head on a rock. Ethan was with him and carried him home." Before noon, the house was filled with people, crowding every room and spilling into the front and back yards both. Tables were set up behind the house, and bowls and platters of food appeared, filled with hominy, deer meat, grape dumplings, eared corn and thick soups.

Emma's father looked handsome and younger than his years.

"He is with his wife, now," they said, to help belie the grief.

On their way home that night, some asked, "What will this do to the wedding?"

"How comfortable can it be, sleeping in a barn?" asked others.

Even, "I wonder if it happened as the stranger said?"

———

Ethan knew—had always known—how they talked when he walked by. Other than a nod of politeness, he avoided Emma for several days after her father's funeral, careful to avoid what could be considered improper.

Emma was alone for the first time in her life. She had no one to tuck her in, no one to tuck in, no one to share her household chores. As she moved from room to room, death spoke to her from every corner. Her mother's Bible. Her father's tools. His boots, his hunting knife.

Loneliness and the crooked-mind way of grief soon got the best of Emma. She found herself slipping into the barn when she knew Ethan was in the fields. Gradually she carried all of her father's tools into the house. *They belonged to him*, she told herself. *No one else should use them.*

One morning Ethan knocked on the back door, "Do you know where the axe might be?" he asked. I need to cut some firewood."

Cut it with your own axe, she almost said, then realized Ethan had no tools of his own. "I am sorry," she said. "Please, I am not thinking. His tools are in the house. Bring them back to the barn." She watched as Ethan carried away her father's tools, and part of her felt as if she were watching a thief in the light of day.

Emma slept lightly when she slept at all. One night she heard footsteps outside her window. Parting the curtains, she saw Ethan slip into the shadows of an elm tree before returning to the barn. The next morning she found his footprints beneath her window.

"Did you sleep well last night?" she asked as she brought him his breakfast.

"Yes, I slept well. Thank you."

"Then why were you lurking around my window?"

Ethan looked at her in surprise before answering. "I chased a bull raccoon," he said. "I kept him from crawling in your window."

"How did you know anything was crawling in my window?"

Ethan took a deep breath and looked to the ground.

"I have been sleeping outside, looking out for you," he said. "Please forgive me. I am only missing you, and I am afraid you will leave me."

That night Emma had a terrifying dream. Ethan crept into her window while she slept, and when she opened her eyes, he stood over her, raising her father's axe as if to strike. She woke up screaming. Ethan pounded on the back door, asking, "Emma, are you alright?"

"Yes," she told him. "Please go."

Thus the days crept by, from dreaded sleep to daytime memories, till Emma's mother showed her strength once more.

———

Emma watched through her window, as she did every night, to assure herself that Ethan retired to the barn. She rolled away from the window and curled her quilt around her cheeks, trembling as she felt herself slipping into darkness. She had only slept a few minutes when she heard a voice.

Emma, wake up sweetheart. It is your mother.

Emma sat up in bed. There stood her mother, wearing her burial dress.

"I want you to see how your father died," she said. "It will not be easy to watch, but it is better you should know."

A soft mist appeared, and Emma watched as Ethan and her father tossed their fishing lines in the creek. She heard Ethan warn him to be careful stepping on the slick stones. She saw Ethan's face writhe in pain as her father fell and struck his head. She saw him carry the old man, pleading and praying and crying as he ran.

"He is a good man, Ethan is," her mother finally said. "He will make a good and faithful husband. Know how he loves you; know how he hurts."

Her mother was soon joined by the ghost of her father. The two stood smiling before her for almost an hour before they drifted away. Emma kept her secret till the noon meal, then told Ethan of the dream. She watched his eyes fill with tears.

"I am ready to be married," she said. "Let them talk if they will. My mother will make them see, if need be."

———

Ethan and Emma were married a month later. As Emma predicted, her mother kept a busy nighttime schedule, readying all for the joy of the wedding day.

Back From the Grave

Whenever the family got together, Grandpaw had one story he always liked to tell. "You know your grandmother came back from the grave, don't you?"

That was a signal we were waiting for. All of us, especially the children, would nod and scoot our chairs real close, or snuggle up to our grandfather on the sofa, and somebody would say, "Why don't you tell us about it, Grandpaw?"

"I believe I might just do that," he'd say, and it seemed like the entire house settled to the ground a few inches just to hear him say it, relieved that Grandmother's memory would once again be with us. Grandpaw's eyes would water over and you could see him drift away to be with her.

"Your grandmother had two things she used to say to me, two things I will never forget. One of those sayings brought her back from the grave. I guess I'll just have to wait to see her in heaven to know which one it was."

"What were they, Grandpaw?" I remember asking.

"The first was this, and she started on me about this just after we got married. I was so impatient, you know, and I loved to eat." He patted his belly as he said this, laughing softly and mostly to himself. This was really funny, because Grandpaw was so skinny his britches were always trying to fall off him, even with that thin-as-a-rope belt he wore squeezed tight enough to leave a scar.

"She'd tell me, hollering, but tenderly, you know, *'Chew your food! Don't just swallow it whole.'* That's good advice for anybody, of course, but there was more to it than that. I think she sometimes thought of me as her little boy, and this let her mother me some."

We laughed to think of Grandpaw as her little boy, giving him the chance to roll the memories around some before he continued. Listening to Grandpaw was always like that. If you didn't just swallow the story, but chewed it real slow, the flavors would linger sweet and delicious.

"The other thing she used to say was this. *'After I die, don't go giving my clothes away. I don't want other ladies wearing my clothes.'* Like I said, I'm not sure which of those sayings brought her back from the grave, but it was one or the other."

"In those old days, we never had much more than what it took to keep us alive. We never had more firewood than we needed to survive the winter. We rarely had more corn than would make a good bowl of soup—and if we did, the neighbors didn't have any, so we'd share with them. Everybody used to, back in those days, just to get along.

"And clothing....well, I'll just tell you this. If I wore a brown shirt, I might as well not have anything on at all, 'cause it would be so threadbare you couldn't tell where the shirt started and my skin left off."

We always laughed when he said that, and some of the boys, without even thinking about it, would let their fingers slide toward their elbows to feel the skin poking through their own threadbare shirts. Some things never seem to change for Indian people.

"So any kind of clothing," Grandpaw continued, "was a special gift, that's for sure. When your grandmother and I had been married for twenty years—and I know that might seem like a long time to you young'uns, but it passed in the blink of an eye—well, six kids and the blink of an eye. Anyways, for that twentieth anniversary I gave your grandmother the most beautiful shawl she or me either one had ever laid eyes on.

"It was woven out of thick cotton fiber and dyed a soft yellow color—not bright yellow like runny egg yolks, more like a faded and more thoughtful yellow, like baby corn when you peel the husk back too early. It had fringe on it, too, deep green fringe that hung three inches all around it. There was nothing all that fancy about it, no beads or trim, just that fringe.

"I didn't wrap it when I gave it to her, just got up from the supper table and went out to the barn where I had it hid. I told her to sit there and not get up. She had that funny little-girl grin on her face when I came back. I was holding the shawl behind my back."

Some of the children wiggled when Grandpaw dragged this part of the story out. They wanted to get to the ghost part, but they knew better than to say anything. This was Grandpaw's time to be with Grandmother, to sit and be with her all over again.

"When I gave it to her I was looking at her eyes. They sparkled and grew big as apples. *'For me?'* she said. 'Of course for you. You are my sweetheart,' I told her. She shook the shawl real gentle, and it floated like a cloud. Your grandmother stood up, wrapped the shawl around her shoulders, and spun so slow I thought the whole house was spinning and she was standing in the middle watching it turn. Your grandmother was very beautiful, you know.

"She wore that shawl to every dance we went to, up to the day she died. I thought about burying her in it. Probably should have, seeing what happened and all. Yes, I can still hear her say, *'After I die, don't go giving my clothes away. I don't want other ladies wearing my clothes.'* I can still hear her say it.

"And that other thing, too. Mercy, yes, I can still hear her say that. *'Chew your food! Don't just swallow it whole.'* I almost died because of that one.

"Your grandmother was a fine cook, you remember. That

deep-dish apple pie she cooked, made from our own back-yard apples, it was my favorite dessert, and she knew it. So while I bought her that shawl for our twentieth anniversary, she cooked me that pie. Two pies! And big ones, too, *'So's you won't go hungry,'* she said, flipping over a towel on the windowsill and showing me the pies. She carried one pie in each hand, like they were gold, incense, and myrrh, and set 'em on the table by my plate.

"I pushed my chicken aside and went after that apple pie. I could see her tightening her lips, like she didn't want to holler at me to slow down, not when I was eating a gifted pie. This just made me go at it faster, and by the time I got to the second pie, without ever slowing down, I dropped the fork and picked up half the pie with both hands. That was all she could stand. She pushed her chair back, stood over me, and hollered, *'Chew your food! Don't just swallow it whole.'*

" 'Even twentieth-anniversary gifted apple pie?' I whimpered. That sent both of us into a laughing spell that lasted for half an hour. I'd grab a piece of pie and she'd chase me around the house like a momma after a thieving little boy. And when we slowed down for a bit, I'd say it again.

" 'Even twentieth-anniversary gifted apple pie?' And off we'd go."

We all laughed and laughed to think of Grandmother chasing Grandpaw around the house like a little boy. I always remember both of them stooping over when they walked through the house, holding onto furniture, walls, and door-ways, but I guess there was a time when they could run.

"It's funny how both of those things, that shawl and the apple pie, had a part in bringing your grandmother back from the grave. I just don't know which one played the biggest part.

"I guess she slowed down quite a bit by the time she died; we both did. But she was still as pretty as ever to me. In a way, I was glad the way she went, the way she just woke up dead one morning. You 'member how I didn't tell anybody till that afternoon?"

Nobody moved a muscle at this part of the story. Whatever Grandpaw did before he told everybody that Grandmother was dead, we wanted him to have a chance to do it all over again.

"Then everyone knew and everyone came over to pay their respects. That's always when the women take over. Some things never seem to change for Indian people," Grandpaw said, laughing, before continuing. "She looked so beautiful lying out there in the front room. I almost expected her to jump up and start filling people's coffee cups. I don't think I really realized she was gone till after she was buried and everybody was gone home, finally back to their own houses and families.

"I know all of you tried your best, dropping by the house like you did, morning, noon, and night. Oh, how I missed your grandmother. After the funeral and the fuss that followed it, one of you'uns finally figured out what would make your grandpaw happy. Apple pie. Always did, always will. Minnie, I think it was, that brought me that pie.

Minnie was my aunt, and when everybody looked at her, she nodded.

"I set the pie up on the windowsill to cool," Grandpaw continued. "I even covered it with a towel to keep the flies off, just like your grandmother would have done. About that time I heard a knocking at the front door. I peeped through the curtain and saw two older Choctaw ladies from down the road. They were too dressed up for social calling. Each lady carried a basket under her arm and they had that begging-for-something set to their jaws.

"I opened the door and asked 'em how I might be of service. 'We are seeking any kind of donations for the poor,' the oldest and purple-dressed one said. 'We thought you might have something special to give in memory of your wife.'

"That was all it took. I never did before or ever-after since cry like that, but something about how they said '*something special in memory of your wife*' sent me into a fit of shaking and crying. I thought they were gonna just leave. They looked awful scared. I shut the door and left them standing there. In not two minutes I came back with your grandmother's shawl in my arms.

" 'This ought to be special enough,' I told them. I kissed it and handed it to the purple one, then shut the door before I changed my mind. After they left, I leaned up against the door for a minute, still struggling to hold back the sobs. That's when I first knew that I was not alone in this house, would never be alone in this house."

When Grandpaw said this, the children shivered and scooted together on the floor. Grandpaw was telling the part they had waited for.

"At first it was like a feeling, like when you know somebody is watching you. Next came the breathing, the soft sound of somebody standing right next to me and breathing. I didn't move, just stayed frozen still. The hair stood up on my neck. Then I heard a sweet little whistling that grew into a breeze. It blew cold on my neck till I shivered all over.

"I worked like a fool the rest of the day. I chopped firewood, I swept the whole house, I cleaned out the chicken coop. I *hated* to clean out the chicken coop.

"By sundown I was exhausted, so I retired to take myself a little nap. I was awakened just after dark by noises coming from the kitchen. It had to be your grandmother. She was shuffling around over by the sink, and I could tell by the way she was making so much noise that she was mad about something. Didn't take me long to figure out what.

'After I die, don't go giving my clothes away. I don't want other ladies wearing my clothes.'

"And there I'd gone and done it. I got up and went to the kitchen, but I didn't see anybody there. Then I saw the apple pie wasn't on the windowsill. Nope, it was setting on the table, with a knife and fork next to it.

"I was so hungry. I ignored the knife, didn't bother with the fork, either. I grabbed a chunk of that pie and bit into it. It dripped sugary apple juice on my chin, but I didn't care. I took another great big bite.

"Then I can't really say what happened exactly, but next thing my teeth turned to rubber and I couldn't chew. I chomped and chomped, but my whole mouth just went dead. I tried to dig the pie out of my throat with my fingers, but it was too deep. I had seen a calf strangle on a birthing cord, so I knew what was happening. I was choking to death.

"I was never afraid of your grandmother before, but when she came into my dying vision, I was flat-out scared to death. She loomed bigger than life over my chair, shaking the chair and looking right in my face. *'Didn't I always tell you? Didn't I? Chew your food! Don't just swallow it whole.'*

"I was so scared I fell over backward, just flopped over on the floor, chair and all. When I did that, the pie popped right out of my mouth. I sucked in all the air I could. Your grandmother was gone by the time I got up, but I knew I'd seen her. She came back to punish me for giving away her shawl, just like I was still her little boy, but she also came back to save me.

"I still miss her," Grandpaw said, "but I know she's watching after me, and that makes missing her a little easier."

Knowing that everybody would soon be moving again, now that his story was over, Grandpaw said, "Maybe this story is about chewing your food, but I don't think so. What do you think?" he asked, turning to the children.

Though nobody said a word, we all knew what the children were thinking. The old ones never leave us. They are still here, all around us. They scold us when we need it and they protect us when we need saving. Some things never seem to change for Indian people.

Tracks in the Mud

"Who do you think did this?"

Billy squeezed his way through the forest of crowded onlookers, slipping under the limbs of wide ladies and around the trunks of stout Chickasaw men.

"Not gonna be easy to figure this one out," said a stoop-shouldered older man, "not with two dozen of us walking all over the killer's tracks."

At the word "*killer*," Billy abandoned all courtesies. He pushed and shoved to get a better look. Kneeling in the mud by the boots of an uncle, he finally could see the object of their stares—a young man lying with his head up against a pile of white stones at the base of a gnarled elm tree.

He looked like a man sleeping on a stone pillow. Sprouting from the skull, long berry-colored streaks wrapped themselves around the white stone.

"Is he dead?" Billy asked.

"Yes, nephew," said the man standing over Billy, smiling in spite of himself to see the determined young boy crouched on the ground beneath him. He reached down and touched Billy's hair and said, "He must have wandered away from the dancing last night. Looks like he either had an enemy or maybe got into a fight with somebody, maybe over a girl. He won't be telling anybody about it."

"He's not from around here, not that I recall," said another uncle.

"Guess we'll find out who he is when his family comes looking for him," said another.

"Maybe he's from over yonder 'cross the south mountain."

Everyone nodded and shrugged, hypnotized to silence at the peaceful beauty and underlying horror of what they beheld. Billy felt tears roll down his cheeks and quiet sobs lifted his tiny chest.

"First time you ever saw anything like this?" the uncle asked.

"Yes," said Billy, wiping his face.

The man knelt down to him and wrapped a strong arm around his shoulders, saying, "This is what sudden death looks like, nephew. It's a part of life. Don't be afraid of it. But don't let it cling to you, either. You are not the dead one. Remember that."

Billy sniffled away the tears and nodded, lying his head against the uncle's shoulder. "Let's see about getting you back home," he said, lifting Billy off his feet and carrying him through the now-thinning crowd.

———

That night, lying on his bed and hoping for good dreams, Billy took a deep breath and closed his eyes with great care. Through the soft cloud of sleep he saw the man on the stone pillow. The man stood up and moved into the darkening shadows, following something into the trees. In the flash of a moment, a deer leapt from the brush and dashed across the clearing.

Billy woke up in a cold sweat, not knowing why the dream left him shaken and afraid. *It was only a deer,* he thought. *A deer followed by a dead man.*

———

The next morning on his way to chop the corn with his father, Billy saw the uncle from the night before, rounding the house and approaching his father. Billy's mother stepped out the back door, wiping her hands on a dish towel.

"I'm Tom McVaney from the old Gardner place," he said,

extending his hand to Billy's father. He touched his hat brim and nodded to Billy's mother. "I come by to see how the boy was. I think he had a scare, seeing the body and all."

"Seem like he's gonna be okay," said Billy's father. "Sometimes he goes where he oughten to."

"My son's the same way, always has been," he said.

"Did they ever find out what happened to that poor boy?" asked Billy's mother.

"Not that I know about, ma'am. Whoever did it must have returned to the dance. All they found in the woods were deer tracks."

"Did he get into a fight with anybody?" asked Billy's father.

"Well, my son Tanchi spoke to him, but nothing come of it. Good day to you folks," McVaney said, turning on his heels and leaving.

Billy stood with his parents and watched Mr. McVaney retreat to the road.

"Nothing come of it," said Billy's mother. "That seems a strange thing to say. Did they argue?"

"He didn't say that," said Billy's father.

"I like him," said Billy. His mother looked at Billy and smiled.

"I'm not saying I don't like him, son. Something is troubling him, is all. That's why he came by this morning. He needs friends." She ruffled Billy's hair and continued. "I think I like him, too. He did right by you, Little Billy."

Billy puffed out his chest and kicked the dirt. He *hated* to be called Little Billy.

———

By evening time everyone in town was speculating about the killing at the dance. Folks gathered on Billy's front porch, sharing the latest rumors and chewing on Billy's mother's famous fried pork.

"It had to be someone at the dance."

"Who ever it is might do it again."

"Wasn't no strangers at the dance, 'cepting for that dead boy. Got to be somebody we know."

"There was that pretty girl," Billy said, remembering a woman from the night before, a young woman in a white dress. "She was a stranger."

All eyes turned to Billy. "Son," said his father. "You need to go in the house."

"Yes, sir," said Billy, standing and slipping through the front door. He knew better. He just forgot. If he kept quiet, he could listen all night, but nobody wanted to hear a boy's opinion.

When he was gone, a neighboring farmer said, "Who was that girl?"

Nobody answered, meaning nobody knew.

"That McVaney boy spent quite a bit of time with her."

"Danced with her three, maybe four times."

"But that was early."

"Yeah. Later on, seemed to me like she had another partner."

"The dead boy. That was her other partner."

"Wonder how Tanchi felt about that?"

Billy listened to the talking through the open window of his bedroom, hoping Mr. McVaney's boy Tanchi wasn't in trouble. He had no way of knowing that the dead man had three older brothers who now were camped on the Canadian River, a half-mile from the McVaney place.

———

When Tanchi left home the next morning in the early dawn, the three brothers met him on the road.

"We need to talk to you," the oldest said.

"What about?" said Tanchi.

"About our brother. What do you know about who killed him?"

"Last I saw, he was leaving the dance with a girl," said Tanchi. "I don't know anything about who killed him. I'm sorry about your loss."

"You follow them?"

"I stayed at the dance. You can ask anybody."

"Anybody in this town would lie for you," said the smallest brother. "We heard you had words with our brother."

"I didn't like him taking my girl, the girl I was dancing with."

"*Your* girl?"

"Look," said Tanchi. "I told your brother I didn't like being played, that's all. The girl only danced with me to make your brother jealous. Once I saw she wasn't interested in me, there was no reason to fight over her."

"Who was the girl?"

"I never saw her before," said Tanchi.

"You know why you're still alive?" said the small brother. Tanchi knew better than to say anything, now that the conversation turned to its true purpose.

"Our father likes to move a little slower than we'd have it," said the oldest. "Just know we are not going anywhere till someone pays for the death of our brother."

———

Two days later the morning fog, thick and wet, hung lower than usual and stayed long enough for six men on horseback to come within a hundred yards of the McVaney spread before they were even spotted. By the time the men reached the house, Tanchi was well on his way to a hunting camp three miles up the river and Mr. McVaney, with his loaded shotgun leaning up against a porch pillar, stood on the front steps to greet them.

"McVaney?" the lead horseman called out.

"Just a minute," said McVaney, disappearing in the house and carrying his gun with him. He knew they would wait five, maybe even ten minutes, before approaching the door. This delay would give Tanchi an extra mile's head start, at least.

When he returned, McVaney said, "How can I help you?"

"We are looking for your son."

"What for?"

The leader swung down from his saddle and took a step forward. "He was one of the last people to speak to my son. I am Hiram Wilson," he said, offering his hand. His manner was friendly, given the circumstances, and McVaney returned his strong handshake and steady gaze.

"My son is not here. He has told his story to your sons and anybody else who'd listen. He and your son did have words, but nothing came of it. Your boy left the dance with a young woman and no one saw him alive after that."

"I did not come to dispute that," said Wilson. "These men are friends of mine and as concerned as I am that my son's killer be brought to justice. We just want to see Tanchi. He danced with the woman. Maybe she saw something. Maybe he knows where we could find her?"

"My son never saw that woman before and never wants to see her again," said McVaney. "She brought bad trouble on our family."

Wilson gestured to a rider wearing overalls and sitting quietly with a straw hat pulled low over his eyes. "Bob Haney here can maybe help us both, if your son has nothing to hide. Get justice for me and freedom from suspicion for your son."

"How can he help us?" said McVaney, and as he spoke the man lifted his head and tilted his hat back. He was an old dark-skinned medicine man, and though McVaney sensed no malice, he knew affairs had taken a serious turn.

"You are a father, like myself," said McVaney, with a visible shudder. He was pleading for not only his son's life, but the well-being of his family for years to come. "I am truly sorry for your loss, sorry it happened, sorry it happened in my town, sorry my boy had anything to do with it. All I ask of you is that you give my son a chance before you do anything to hurt him."

"What do you want?"

"Only that you find out all you can before Bob Haney goes for my boy. Look for the truth."

"You have my word on that," said Wilson, looking at Haney as he spoke. "I don't imagine you want to tell us where your son might be."

"You know I can't do that. If you want to know about your boy's death, I can show you the dance grounds."

"We'd be grateful."

Soon McVaney and the six horsemen were riding north, headed for the pine woods at the base of Red Mountain.

———

By the time they reached the dance grounds, a dozen men from town were waiting, alerted by Mrs. McVaney. The men glared at each other as some dismounted and huddled in pairs, while others chose to stay near their guns. McVaney led Bob Haney and Wilson through the yellowing sycamore trees to the spot where the body was found.

The two fathers stood on the edge of the clearing and watched as Haney circled the trees, kneeling to touch the tracks in the mud before approaching the white stones. He crouched down, closed his eyes, and waited for a moment before slowly stretching out his right hand to touch the stones. With a move as natural as a wave, Haney lifted his left palm to the sky and held it there for several minutes. In a flicker of unseen time, he stood between the two men.

"Mr. Wilson," he said, "that McVaney boy had nothing to do with this killing. You need to be looking for that woman they danced with."

Hiram Wilson dropped his jaw and looked wide-eyed at Haney, wanting to protest, but the old man had already turned his back and was walking briskly to the horses.

———

In those days the dancing came once a month, and with all the medicine-making and asking and denying, all to the unalterable pace of Indian Time, dance Saturday soon came again. Death and dying being a regular part of living in the old days; nobody thought of not having the dance. Folks who had not attended a dance in years came, some traveling for fifty miles and camping over for several days.

Billy had formed the comical habit of putting both hands over his mouth, pressing his lips together, and mumbling "*ummm*" for several minutes at a time whenever he was tempted to talk in the presence of adults, knowing his father would use any excuse to make him stay home from the dance. When his father guided their wagon to the usual spot in the shade of an elm grove, Billy saw that the horses of the Wilson brothers were already tethered there. Though his father said nothing, Billy knew by his jerky movements in tying the horses that he was worried.

Billy's favorite part of the dance was just after sundown, when the fire was crackling high and the flaming shadows were big as trees. Like red and yellow spirits, the shadows danced their own dance, flickering on tree trunks and across the sweating faces, all to the screech of sweet Indian fiddles and deep-voiced singing.

The Wilson brothers stood like stubborn adversaries, talking too loudly and swaggering too close to the dancing. Tanchi stayed across the grounds from them, but as the evening progressed and they continued to point at him, the trouble grew with every twitch of the lead fiddler's bow, till the youngest brother walked through the dancers and approached Tanchi.

Though nobody stopped their dancing and the glances were subtle, everyone watched and waited for blows to be struck. Billy had spent most of the evening playing a toss-stone game by himself, never out of sight of Tanchi, his new big brother, and Mr. McVaney, his new favorite uncle. From his seat on the ground behind the tree where Tanchi stood, Billy heard every word spoken between the Wilson boy and his friend.

Billy also saw a dark figure emerging from the depths of the woods, from the clearing of death, lured by the smells and sounds of living people dancing. He saw the woman. She was dressed in a white buckskin dress, decorated with thin crimson streaks that ran from the shoulders to the ground.

Tanchi and the dead man's brother, leaning far too close to each other for friendly talking, did not see her.

"You think you got away with killing our brother?"

"I didn't kill nobody."

"So just because an old man says you didn't, you think we are fooled. Our father, maybe, but not me and my brothers. The time will come; we got our eyes on you."

Tanchi said nothing, just kept his hands in his pockets and his eyes on the ground. The Wilson boy saw the woman before Tanchi did.

"That the girl you was dancing with?" he asked, pointing over Tanchi's shoulder. Tanchi turned and before he could speak, the Wilson boy pushed him aside and sidled up to the woman, who stood in the shadows, unseen by the others.

The woman reached her hand out to him and said, "I was hoping you would come tonight."

"Let me get my brothers. We have plenty to talk to you about," he said.

"Later we can talk," the woman said. "Don't worry. We have all evening. I'll tell you whatever you like."

The young man stood confused. Billy knew by the way he looked at the soft flow of her white buckskin dress, the youngest Wilson boy could be led anywhere by this strange and powerful woman.

Had Billy been a year older and less comfortable crawling about on the ground, he would never have noticed, but he was barely ten years old, and so he saw. Beneath the hem of the woman's dress were the thin, lean legs and hooves of a deer.

The sight of the dead man came at him in a flood of memory, the deep bruises and cuts on his face and neck, the cracked skull that led all to believe only a strong young man, a man like Tanchi, could inflict such wounds.

"No tracks in the mud leading away from the dance," the men had said. "Only deer tracks." Everyone thus believed the killer had returned to the dance.

Deer Woman, thought Billy. *She is the killer.*

She now held the Wilson boy by both hands and was slowly backing through the sycamore trees and to the clearing where the white stones still dripped crimson.

"Tanchi," Billy yelled. "Don't let them go!"

Tanchi flung a quick and startled look at Billy. "How long have you been here?" he asked.

"Look at her," Billy said. "Look at her legs. She is a deer woman. She is the killer."

Hearing his cries, the crowd left their dancing and followed Billy and Tanchi to the clearing, where the Deer Woman was already stomping the fallen Wilson boy to the ground. A rifle shot exploded and the woman fled into the woods.

Tom McVaney lowered his gun and went to the Wilson boy, who lay on the stones, bleeding and wounded but alive.

———

A man of more normal ambitions than Hiram Wilson, a man more inclined to familial tenderness, might well have survived the death of one son and the near death of the other at the hands of a supernatural seductress. But the added humiliation of having his youngest son saved by Tom McVaney, Tanchi's father, was too much crow for a proud man to swallow.

Neither McVaney nor anybody else in town ever saw Hiram Wilson again.

The talk was that he became a recluse in his grief and was never the same, leaving the running of his farm to hired hands, who stole from him until the family fortunes dwindled and his living sons were forced to make their own way in the world.

To those tempted to blame the seductress, consider this. Deer Women come when Deer Women are called. It is their nature.

Regarding Billy, he would never forget the happenings of that summer; his first view of death, his discovery that blessings *can* come from listening, and his first true awakening to the river of love that flows between good parents and their children.

Rabbit Death

John Perry was a loner. On hunting trips, as soon as the young hunters made camp, Perry would disappear into the woods, avoiding the others and stalking game in silence. For most hunters, these trips were more about being together and shooting arrows with friends than killing game, for deer are easily frightened by loud boys in bunches. But John Perry was not interested in being with anyone.

"John is just not good with people," his own mother often said.

"He's a good hunter," his father would reply.

Perry would rather hunt than be with people, who frightened him and made him feel clumsy. He was especially good at catching rabbits, and was often able to track them by the loose brush scattered about the base of bushes or even the smell of their droppings. He usually killed enough rabbits to feed everyone in camp, sometimes even more than the hunters could eat.

One day Perry had already killed more than a dozen rabbits and was returning to camp with his latest batch when he heard the tiny squeals of baby rabbits in a small hole at the base of an old cypress tree near a sweet-water spring. He knelt and cupped a handful of water. The mother rabbit leapt noisily in front of him, crisscrossing back and forth before dashing into the woods.

"She wants to lead me away from her babies," thought Perry. "Alright, I will wait for her." He crept into the nearby bushes and sat so still even the mother rabbit thought he had gone and her babies were safe.

When he saw the mother rabbit step into the opening and sniff the air, Perry hit her in the back of the neck with an arrow. She leapt three feet in the air and flipped on her back on the ground, squealing a high-pitched scream and panting away her life.

Perry stood over her and watched her shivering in the throes of death.

He turned to the tree and stared at the hole, hoping another rabbit would bound through the bushes and try to lure him away, but the bushes were silent. The black rabbit hole seemed to grow in accusation. Perry fell to his knees and crawled through the underbrush to the base of the tree, then parted the leaves and slipped his hand through the opening.

He felt warm fur squirming and wiggling in his palm. Pulling his hand from the hole, Perry smiled and spoke to the rabbits.

"Don't be afraid, little friends." He laid the four tiny rabbits in his lap and watched them roll against each other, nuzzling in the circle of warmth. As he imagined what they would look like as adult rabbits, the slow realization crossed his mind that he was not their friend at all. Instead, he was their worst enemy. He was more powerful than they would ever be and he held their death in his hands. He had already slain their mother, and for no cause.

The baby rabbits were barely able to open their eyes. They snuggled into the comfort of each other and Perry carefully placed them back in the hole.

———

"Where have you been?" asked his friends when Perry returned to the camp that night.

"I was hunting," he said.

"Hunting? Maybe you should give the rabbits a day off," someone said, and everyone laughed.

"Yeah, what happens when there are no rabbits left?" said another, and the laughter continued.

"There are rabbits left," said Perry. "I just saw four baby rabbits down by the spring."

"You saw four rabbits and you didn't kill them?" As the ribbing shifted from one boy to another, Perry quietly made his way into the woods. He slept away from the others that night, and before sunrise he made his way to the cypress tree and the hole beneath it. In the soft yellow of coming dawn he saw four tiny firefly lights float from the hole. They flitted around his face until he brushed them away.

Perry reached into the hole and felt the warm rabbits. He smiled and rolled their tiny bodies on his palm before lifting them from the hole. His smile soon froze on his face. The rabbits lay on his hand without moving. Life had left the rabbits only a moment before.

Perry cupped his other hand over the rabbits and sobbed. His body shook with the deep cries of a young boy questioning, for the first time, his pride in killing.

"Perry?" He looked up to see Arnie Sam, the youngest of his friends. "Are you crying?"

"No," said Perry. "I was blowing into this hole to see if more rabbits will run out. I've already killed some."

"Let me see them," said Arnie.

"Go home!" said Perry, ashamed to yell at Arnie, but more ashamed of the dead rabbits. "You talk too much. You scare the rabbits."

Arnie hung his head and walked away.

———

The next morning Perry told his mother, "Maybe I'll stay home today and hunt squirrels close to the house."

"Are you feeling alright?" his mother asked.

Perry did not reply, but by midday his mother saw a red

skin rash creeping from his hands to his chest. She sent word for an *alikchi*, a good doctor.

"Where have you been for the past few days?" the *alikchi* asked.

"Hunting. I always go hunting."

"Rabbit hunting?"

"Yes," said Perry.

"You have caught a sickness from the rabbits. You have touched too much death."

The *alikchi*, the town doctor, called for a *pashofa* dance, a healing dance. All day Perry's mother and the women of the town cooked the thick corn soup, *pashofa*. The *alikchi* called together his helpers, and the dancing began before sundown. Through the night the singers chanted and the dancers stepped their healing steps. They took breaks as the night wore on and the *pashofa* was available for everyone.

When morning came, the *alikchi* said, "There is nothing more I can do now. We should wait and see if the healing takes place."

The rash grew till it covered Perry's body with red sores. The itching spread over his back and belly, even under his hair. Perry rolled over in his sleep, trying to find a spot that did not sting. His friends stopped coming by to ask for him.

"Better stay away from that Perry," their parents warned. "He caught that disease and you might catch it, too."

One day Arnie walked by Perry's house, crossing the street to the other side as his mother told him to. Perry looked through his window and called to him.

"Arnie! Want to talk?"

"Sure," said Arnie, eager to have an excuse to see his friend. He walked to the door, but Perry said, "Maybe you should come to the window. We can visit from here."

Arnie sat beneath the window, and though they spoke

only a few words, the two friends visited for half an hour. Arnie knew that Perry must look too bad to want anyone to see him. Finally he said, "I should be going."

"Want to come by tomorrow?" asked Perry.

"Sure," said Arnie. "When are you going to be well?"

"Probably tomorrow. If not, the next day," Perry said. When Arnie was gone, Perry rolled over and cried. His face was a swollen mass of red sores. He knew if any of his friends saw him this way, they would speak his name in whispers as if he were already dead.

That night an owl came to Arnie's window, screeching his death call. Arnie's parents chased the owl away and lit a cedar torch to smoke his room.

"Did you see Perry?" his mother asked.

"Yes," said Arnie. "But I did not go in his home."

"Then maybe this is a warning," she said. "You stay away from Perry's house or you'll bring death on this family."

"I am sorry. I have missed him and he called to me from the street."

"We all miss Perry," she said. "You must understand he may never be healed."

The next day Arnie was walking by the graveyard and saw four baby rabbits playing in the grass. He ran to them, then stopped when he saw they were running back and forth on the gravesite of Perry's grandfather, close to where Perry would someday be buried. As Arnie watched, the rabbits stopped running and rolled on their backs. They shivered and squealed, then lay still as stones.

Arnie knelt to the rabbits, but before he touched them, the air cracked with the harsh cry of a snow owl. He looked to the sky and rose to his feet. Arnie ran home that day, but not before looking over his shoulders and seeing four large lights rise from the bodies of the dead rabbits.

Spirits, he thought. *Graveyard spirits.*

That night strange dogs came from the graveyard and walked down the center of the street howling. When they came to Perry's house, they stood in the yard and yelped and hollered till his father fired a rifle at them. The dogs disappeared but the howling continued for more than an hour.

Every night for a week the unseen dogs howled, and on the morning when Perry finally died, the four lights came from the graveyard to carry him away. Perry's mother found him lying limp on the floor beside his bed. He was as thin as a child half his age, loose skin stretched over a skeleton of bones.

"Why did Perry die?" Arnie asked his mother after the funeral.

"Only Perry knows that," she said. "The way he never seemed to fight death, surely he knew."

"I hope he also knew I was his friend," said Arnie.

"Oh, he knew that. Everyone could see you were his friend."

Arnie's mother spoke the truth. Everyone could see that Arnie was Perry's friend, including Perry.

A fortnight after the burial, Perry returned. He brought the four baby rabbits to see Arnie, who first heard the footsteps on his porch. Someone then walked through his front door and stopped outside his bedroom.

"Arnie?" came the faint call.

"Yes."

"Open the door, Arnie."

Arnie cracked open the door and there sat four rabbits, tucked in the cotton cloth lining a cane basket. Arnie lifted the basket from the floor, but before he closed his door, he saw Perry smiling, standing in the shadows with his hands covering his face.

"Please let me see," said Arnie. "I promise not to be afraid."

Perry lifted his hands slowly and with a fearful look in his eyes. His skin was clean.

"You look good," said Arnie. "Ready for the trip. Your mother would be proud to see your face. Don't worry about the rabbits, either. I'll see that they live."

Perry nodded and vanished into the dark of the night. He did make one final stop before making his death journey. His mother heard a chair leg scraping on the kitchen floor and rose to find Perry sitting in his chair with an empty bowl in front of him. She filled it with *Pashofa* and sat by him as he took his final spoonful before sinking into the gray dawn.

The Jealous Witch

Bertha's chickens were plump and happy. They cackled endlessly, unaware that their very plumpness, a source of such joy and pride, would soon consign them to the chopping block. Bertha talked to her chickens. She loved them and was even known to shed a tear when company was coming and fried chicken seemed the obvious entrée.

On such days she would sharpen her axe, grab a favorite hen by the legs with her left hand, and carry the writhing chicken to the knee-high, blood-splattered stump. With a quick downward thrust of the silvery blade, she would send the chosen victim's head flailing across the yard, as the hen's incredulous eyes beheld their betrayer. Following a pot of boiling water for plucking and a hot pan of grease for frying, the hen left Bertha's home resting comfortably in the bellies of several smiling Chicasaw men.

"That Bertha can cook!" men said.

"She can raise a fine hen as well," the women echoed. Everybody loved Bertha.

———

Maybe that was the problem. When everybody loves somebody, it won't be long before somebody gets jealous. Bertha never deliberately did anything to bring attention to herself, other than serve the best meal she knew how, whether it was bright yellow-yoked eggs for breakfast or the afore-mentioned fried chicken for dinner. She did sing throughout the day, but who could blame anyone for that?

A witch, that is who—a jealous witch.

Bertha began noticing small mishaps that had never

happened before. First her hog fat was dirty, and when she plopped a spoonful into a pan of scrambled eggs, the crunchy dirt spread amongst the eggs. Luckily, Bertha always tasted any dish before she served it, so the waste was only the six eggs and not her reputation. When a prize rooster flapped his wings, crowed a last crow, and fell over dead one morning, Bertha knew she had a serious problem.

She cried a long and heartfelt cry that day, just sat on her back porch and wiped her cheeks and sniffled, knowing her peaceful days were over. An hour after the grim discovery of the dead rooster, Bertha stood up, wiped her face with her apron, and made a firm decision.

Her best friend from childhood, Ruthie Lee, had moved into her aunt's house. The house sat downriver from Tishomingo and stood by itself for two miles around. Bertha seldom saw Ruthie Lee these days, but she knew the path she had taken. Ruthie Lee could be a friend to some and a deeply feared enemy to others. She made her living, or at least the cash portion of it, peddling love potions to the boys looking for romance.

After a fitful night spent wide-awake with her shotgun in the chicken yard, Bertha saddled her horse and began the long trip to Ruthie Lee's place.

Ruthie Lee met her at the door after the six-hour trip and without even a hello, asked Bertha, "What would you like me to do exactly?"

"Good to see you, too," said Bertha.

"Oh," said Ruthie Lee, "I don't mean to be rude. I just wanted to get along with helping you in your business."

"Well, I don't want anybody killed," said Bertha. "I just want the life I had, a happy life for me and my chickens both."

"You know better than that, Bertha. The life you know is no more, not once the witching starts."

"Can't blame me for hoping," Bertha replied with a sigh.

"Nope, I won't hold that against you. Now, what's your thinking on the matter?"

"I don't know why anyone would take after me," said Bertha.

"No trouble with anybody?"

"No."

"Think on it, now," said Ruthie Lee.

"None, not that I recall."

"No troubles at all, with nothing or nobody?" asked Ruthie Lee.

"None."

"Well, there's your answer, then."

"Huh?"

"If you are living such a happy and trouble-free life, you've gone and made somebody jealous," said Ruthie Lee.

Bertha eased herself to a sitting position on the front step, sliding her hand along the pine support. "Can you help me?"

"Yes. Are you sure you want my help?"

"I don't want any more dead chickens."

"You mean you don't want anyone *else* killing your chickens," laughed Ruthie Lee.

Bertha eyed her friend with a sly grin.

"Fine," said Ruthie Lee. "Go on home. It's taken care of. If you want to know who's been troubling you, look out the window at dawn tomorrow."

"Anything I should do?" asked Bertha.

"Well, there is one thing. You might pour buckets of water on your chicken yard. Make it a real mess, the muddier the better."

———

Exhausted from the long journey, Bertha enjoyed a quick nap before going about the task of emptying twenty buckets of well water on the soft dirt of her chicken yard. She then settled in a chair by the kitchen window, with her loaded shotgun and a good clean view of the ankle-deep muddy yard and the woods beyond.

She woke herself with her own snoring an hour before dawn, and sat up rubbing her eyes and hoping she had not missed anything. Tempted to inspect her chicken coop for dead hens or roosters, she gripped the chair instead, realizing her house was probably watched at this very minute by the eyes of her evil tormentor.

As the pink streaks of sunlight colored the horizon, Bertha saw a shadowy figure moving from the trees in the direction of her yard. She knelt to the floor and peered over the top of her windowsill. There was old Hazel Redwing, lifting her dress and sneaking across the pasture.

"That prune-faced old witch!" said Bertha, clapping her hand over her mouth as Hazel paused and looked to the house. Satisfied she was undetected, Hazel continued her sly walking to the chicken yard.

From her position at the window, Bertha watched as Hazel stopped and stared, dropping her jaw and wrinkling her brow. Bertha pulled back the curtain to get a better look. Six fat hens stood perched on the low-slung roof overlooking the yard, standing shoulder to shoulder and leaning their heads at Hazel as if readying for attack. The lead hen lifted her leg and flashed what looked to Bertha like a razor-sharp chicken foot.

Hazel must have seen the same, for she lifted her arms to her face to wield off the onslaught. The six hens flapped their wings and flew at Hazel. She turned to run, but tripped in the muddy soup of the yard. With an eerie squawk, Hazel flung her arms and lifted herself from the ground, flying to the woods in the form of an owl.

Bertha leaned against the kitchen wall and thought for long moments, replaying what she had witnessed. Her chickens were safe, her tormentor vanquished, never to return. Of this she felt assured.

So why am I feeling so uncomfortable?

"I don't want any more dead chickens," she recalled telling Ruthie Lee, and Ruthie Lee had granted her request.

So why am I feeling so uncomfortable?

She now recalled the irony in Ruthie Lee's reply: "You mean you don't want anyone *else* killing your chickens."

Bertha's chickens were safe, but they also appeared to be armed.

What happens when they realize Hazel is a recent enemy, but I've been killing their kin for a decade? she thought.

_____

Two hours later, when she summoned the courage to enter her own chicken yard, Bertha found Hazel's shoes, stuck in the black water and mud. She stored them away in her closet, knowing that as long as she had them Hazel would never bother her again.

_____

The real trial came the following day when a cousin stopped by for dinner.

"That is the best meal I've had in years," her cousin said, wiping the grease from his lips. "But I have to admit, Bertha, I was a little disappointed when I saw what you were serving."

Bertha just beamed and he continued.

"Yes, your fried chicken is legendary, and when I saw that platter of pork steaks, I thought maybe you didn't like me no more. But mercy, Bertha, that has to be the best pork I've ever tasted."

"Why thank you," said Bertha. "I think from now on I'll be serving quite a bit of pork. It's just so much more versatile than chicken, I'm thinking lately."

_____

From that day forward her chickens remained plump and happy, cackling in endless conversation with their new friend Bertha.

Creek Stories

Today the capital of the Muscogee Creek Nation is located in Okmulgee, Oklahoma, and boasts 30,000 enrolled members. According to Muscogee origin stories, the people settled in the southeast after a long-ago migration from lands in the west. Creek settlements were permanent villages situated along river valleys in the modern-day states of Georgia and Alabama. A ceremonial plaza, used for games, religious ceremonies, and social events, stood at the center of the village. The people lived in wooden huts with grass or wood-shingle roofs.

Once a year, the larger mother villages hosted the Green Corn Ceremony. This was a time to forgive disagreements with other tribal members as a way of renewing and strengthening community bonds. During the several days of the ceremony, old household items were thrown out, dwellings were thoroughly cleaned, and the Sacred Fire was rekindled by the High Priest. Following the ceremony, participating Creeks returned to their smaller daughter villages carrying embers from the ceremonial fire. This created among the Creeks the strong belief that they all shared one common fire.

In native Creek beliefs, all of creation was attributed to the "Maker of Breath." Creek society was divided into a number of groups, or clans, and each clan was associated with a particular animal. For example, the Panther Clan is linked to the panther, the first animal created by Breath Maker and given considerable strength and spiritual power. Other clan names are Bear, Wind, Deer, Bird, Fox, Snake, Beaver, Mink, Alligator, Skunk, Buzzard, Rabbit, and Raccoon.

Creeks believed that man and wild animals could speak with each other and be understood. In the stories "Long-Clawed One" and "The Hunters' Wives," dogs speak to warn their masters of impending death. The Creek woods were full of animal spirits, and hunters prayed before killing an animal, such as a deer, so as not to offend the spirits.

As in many of the southeastern cultures, snakes were an important source of immense power and ominous danger. Many stories tell of snakes that possess potent magic and the dangers associated with trying to obtain their power. Objects such as colored stones, crystals, or special dolls are also known to possess strong medicine-magic, usually as protection from the dark and mysterious forces.

Shape-shifting witches and other magical beings prowled the dense forests of Creek lore, hungry for human flesh. Sometimes appearing as human, other times as common animals, these malevolent creatures moved in and out of communities, barely noticed. It should be noted that for Native Americans, witches did not resemble the European broom riders of western folklore.

So strong was the belief in witchcraft among traditional Creeks that a doctor whose patient died was likely to be accused of witchcraft. In some cases, the doctor himself would be put to death. Witches were believed to fly great distances to poison their perceived enemies. This poisoning could consist of merely blowing contagious air into a house by flying by at night, or breathing lethal air into a person's lungs while he slept.

Creeks have always believed a good life would be rewarded, and Creek stories reflect this belief. The hard-working younger brother suffers much ridicule from his older siblings in "Panther Man," but his efforts thwart his sister's death. Conversely, ignoring the warnings and taking a darker path can lead to painful change or death, as in the poignant story "Two Friends."

Today, as in the past, many Creek stomp dancers sing and dance around a seasonal fire in sacred ceremonies. Stomp grounds are thriving, and modern Creeks still cleanse their stomp grounds before performing the ancient dances. Today the Creek people belong to two factions: the traditional and those professing Christianity. Oklahoma Creeks and those residing on the Poarch Creek Indian Reservation in Atmore, Alabama, are experiencing a strong revival of interest in lore and language; and Creek writers are earning well-deserved respect in the academic world of American letters.

Two Friends

They say that opposites attract, and the friendship of Longbow and Treestump was a classic example. Longbow was tall and lean and often seemed to disappear inside himself with thought.

"He is a brooding one," the women said.

"He looks unhappy."

"Why doesn't he talk more?'

"Maybe there aren't any words left over after Treestump has finished talking," Spiceycorn said. All the others laughed and nodded.

"Yes, that Treestump, he's the funny one."

"He is a happy fellow, always singing."

"Always getting into something."

"And he will try anything."

"Yes, he will try anything. Maybe he needs to learn something from his Longbow friend. Maybe he should try listening." The women thought for a moment, pausing with their fingers from shucking the corn.

"But I still can't stop laughing when I think of Treestump," Spiceycorn said. Everyone smiled and rocked for a while in the memory boat of Treestump's antics before gradually returning to work.

———

As the boys grew older, they were inseparable. They always ran together, the one tall, lean, and thoughtful, the other round and happy, always trying new things. Longbow was the cautious one, more apt to examine every angle before acting.

Once the boys ran to the edge of a big boulder over-looking a deep pool. Longbow stayed carefully away from the ledge, while Treestump leaned over and peered at the water far below.

"Look at the splash I can make," said Treestump.

"You don't know where the bottom is," warned Longbow. "You've never jumped from this place before."

"Nothing's going to hurt me." Treestump dashed to the boulder's edge and leapt, waving his arms and shouting as he fell. When he struck the pool he showered Longbow with water. Longbow took off his shirt, laid it on the boulder to dry, and climbed down the boulder to the shore. He dipped his foot in the water. He waded into the water, swam to the center, and touched the bottom in several places before he felt safe enough to jump from the high boulder.

When he did jump, he arched his back and dove into the pool, making barely a ripple on the water's surface. Treestump stood and watched, and when his friend climbed out of the water, he said, "Nice dive. But running and jumping is more fun."

As the years passed, Longbow grew even taller and his long legs developed strong, lean muscles. He became a fine runner. Everyone came to the races to see how far Longbow would stretch the distance between himself and his closest competitor. Treestump sometimes was so far behind he would step off the racing course and no one would even notice.

One day Treestump took a shortcut through the woods. As Longbow was streaking toward the finish, in the lead as usual, Treestump leapt out of the woods and began flipping and turning comical somersaults all across the finish line. Winded as he was from the long race, Longbow had to stop and laugh. The women who had watched the race had plenty to say, as usual.

"See how he makes fun, even now as his friend is winning."

"He can't run, but he's a funny one."

"He makes me laugh to look at him."

"Everybody likes Treestump."

"That Treestump, he's a happy fellow."

"That Treestump, maybe he's a jealous fellow," Spiceycorn said.

And so it went. Longbow became ever quieter, more the listener. When the two grew old enough, they camped far away from the others on hunting trips, and always returned with a deer. Though Longbow shared the credit, very seldom did Treestump make the kill.

Secretly Treestump wished he could be tall and lean. He longed to be a swift runner, a good hunter, but not enough to stop talking and joking. He loved to make people laugh; that was his nature.

———

One night as the two were camping and finishing their meal of fish, Longbow said, "An old man came to the camp last week. I think you saw him."

"Yeah, I saw him. He had a beautiful horse," said Treestump.

"Did you listen to him? Did you hear what he said?" asked Longbow.

"No, he was a strange one. He talked in mysteries. I didn't hear what he said. I didn't listen."

"Well," said Longbow, "he said there was a way for people to change. It's not always safe. In fact, he talked of changing into a snake, a long, lean snake."

"Changing into a snake!" said Treestump. "Ha, like you! You are like a snake."

"No," said Longbow. "No, I am not like a snake."

"A skinny snake," insisted Treestump. "Yes, you are. A skinny snake. You slither in and out of the ladies' dreams. I see how they look at you."

The two friends laughed.

"Yes," Longbow said, laughing nervously. "He told how to do it. He said you cook the brains of a black squirrel, and the brains of a black snake, and the brains of a wild turkey. You chop them and stir them all together and fry them, maybe with onions. When you eat them…"

"Was he serious?" asked Treestump. "He told you how to become a snake?"

Longbow stopped laughing and looked at his friend. "We don't want to think about this."

"Yes, we do. What else did he say?" asked Treestump.

"He said you have to be careful." When he saw how serious Treestump was in his listening, Longbow said, "He said nothing. I was making it all up."

"You are not making it up. Tell me!"

Treestump began to wrestle with Longbow. He pushed him to the ground, leapt on top of him, and pinned his arms down.

"Tell me!" he said, and though he was laughing, he knew his knees were digging into his friend's lean arm muscles. He saw the pain on Longbow's face. "You can tell me," said Treestump. "I'll let you up if you'll tell me."

"Then you'll never know," said Longbow.

Treestump laughed and rolled aside. Longbow rose slowly to a sitting position.

"Thank you for letting me up," said Longbow. His voice was deep and menacing, like a slow-spreading fire. "I will tell you what the man said. He said you chop them up fine and you fry them over a hot fire. Eat these brains and you will become a black snake, a long, thin black snake."

Before Longbow knew what was happening, Treestump

had jumped to his feet and disappeared into the woods, carrying only his hunting knife. In less than an hour, he returned with everything, the black squirrel, the black snake, and the turkey.

"Help me," he said, tossing his catch at Longbow. "We've got to clean and fry the brains."

"You should not be doing this," said Longbow.

"Help me, don't be lazy."

"I am not lazy. I am being your friend."

"A friend would help another friend."

"Not to get in trouble. Not to hurt himself."

Treestump didn't reply. He just worked away, cutting and chopping. With two stones he banged through the skull and took the brains.

"Help me with a fire," he said. "At least build a fire."

"What do you want with a fire?"

"You know what I want with a fire. I'm frying these brains. I'm cooking them, just like the man said to do."

"I told you what the man said not to do. I will not help you build a fire." Treestump worked while his friend walked behind him, challenging him.

"You know better. You should not be doing this."

"I shouldn't do this? You are the tall one. You are the fast one. You are the handsome one, the good hunting one. What am I? I am like the stump of a tree. People sit on me. They laugh at me. They use me like a treestump. That's why they call me that. I roll and somersault and make the funny jokes, and look at you."

"People love you," said Longbow. "You could make far less jokes than you do and they would still love you. There is no need to make a fool of yourself."

Treestump gathered wood for the fire, brushing against his friend without replying, so Longbow continued. "How do you think I feel? People look at me and shake their heads and wonder why I have nothing to say. I have nothing to say because . . . I have nothing to say. I am not clever like you are."

Treestump refused to listen. He stoked the fire with dry leaves and small twigs until the leaves were crackling and hissing. He set a small pan on the fire and fried the meat. The brains sizzled and shrank, smelling sweet and rich.

And so they sat, the two. Treestump pierced the brains with a long, green branch he had cut from a nearby tree. Gray and green smoke rose into the swampy air, curling and twisting. It seemed as if their lives were curling and twisting also, slowly changing as the green smoke dissolved in the thick air of the swamp.

"You shouldn't do this," said Longbow. "You know better than to do this. If I were not your friend, if I did not respect you so, I might grab the stick and hurl it into the swamp. Maybe that's what a friend would do." He wrapped his arms around himself and said, over and over, shaking as he said it, "You shouldn't do this. You shouldn't do this."

"You could grab the stick," said Treestump. "You could hurl the stick. You could run away with it. You can outrun me. You are quicker than I am. But now that I know that brains and fire are all that's needed to change, you can't be with me always."

So they sat. Longbow turned away when his friend began to eat. An hour later, Treestump lay with his blanket pulled over him. The sun was gone, and the air of the swamp grew thick. The night noises hummed with a loud music, a music made of unseen creatures moving in the shadows, the plopping and splashing in the water, the sliding and scraping on the shoreline, the calling of the night birds, pierced by the screams of unknown things from deep in the swamp where sunlight never fell.

With his blanket pulled up to his chin, Treestump said, "Longbow."

"Yes."

"I am beginning to change."

"You may think it is funny," said Longbow. "But you didn't see the strange man. You didn't listen to the man. He wasn't smiling. You didn't see how the old men looked at him when he talked. They respected him, but they were scared of him, too. They knew his magic was heavy and thick. I should never have told you. You think it's all a joke."

"I don't think it's a joke at all," Treestump said. "I am changing."

Longbow stood up and walked to his friend. "How are you changing? Tell me what I can do."

"My feet," he said. "Will you pull my boots off?"

Longbow knelt and lifted the blanket from his friend's feet.

"No!" said Treestump. "Keep my feet covered. Just pull my boots off." Longbow grabbed the boots by the heels, one at a time, and tugged and removed them.

"That feels better," said Treestump. "I think it is alright. I don't think I am changing after all. My stomach is sick. That meat was no good. That's all. Let's go to sleep."

Longbow returned to his blanket and soon was sound asleep.

———

Treestump rolled over and over in his sleep, waking often and remembering what he had done, hoping it was all a dream. Once he slipped his fingers beneath the covers and felt scales growing up his calf, covering his knees, and climbing to his waist. He started to call out to Longbow.

There is nothing Longbow can do, he realized. *He already warned me. He did everything he could to stop me.*

Treestump hoped that by making a fire and sitting in the cedar smoke, the dark snake magic would turn away. *If I can talk Longbow into hunting without me, I can throw the blanket back once he is gone. The bright sunshine, together with the fire, will bring my own skin back. The scales will flake away.*

―――

An hour before sunrise, Longbow heard his friend shuffling and scraping the embers of the fire. With his blanket clutched around his knees, Treestump was crawling on the ground and moving in a strange way. With great effort, he rolled a log onto the fire.

"Oh, I'm sorry," said Treestump. "I thought you were asleep."

"I was. You woke me up. Should be a good day for hunting. Looks like the cloud cover will stay. The deer should be out."

"Yes."

"How do you feel?"

"I feel fine. I think I will stay here while you hunt this morning. Maybe I'll go this afternoon."

Longbow got up and sat with his friend by the fire. "You sure you feel okay?"

"Of course I feel okay. It's just my stomach that doesn't feel so well. I'll be fine."

"I'll stay with you," said Longbow. "I'll wait till you feel better and we can both go hunting."

"No, please," said Treestump. "I would feel awful keeping you from hunting. You go."

So Longbow left his friend sitting by the fire.

―――

When Longbow returned from the hunt, he found Treestump lying next to the water with his blanket pulled up around his chin. His neck looked dark, as if his skin had developed a rash.

"How are you? How do you feel?" asked Longbow.

"I have something to tell you, Longbow. Don't touch me, please. And don't stare at me. Come sit by me."

"What is it?" said Longbow, sitting next to his friend.

"I am changing, like I said last night. When you pulled my boots off I could feel the change. It never stopped."

"What kind of change?"

"Please," said Treestump. "Just listen. I only want to say it once. I think the change is coming quickly. I am becoming a snake. The scales have climbed up. I have no arms. What you see above my neck is what is left of me. The rest is already a snake."

Longbow reached to grab the blanket.

"No! No!" said Treestump. "You will see soon enough. I had hoped the sun or the fire or the cedar smoke could drive it away, but you were right. The magic is strong. I want to lie here, if I can. I want to spend my last hour as a person with you."

And so he did. Longbow watched in silence as one square of skin after another hardened and turned to scales. As the skin of Treestump's face gradually took on a darker hue and seemed to crack before his eyes, Longbow turned his head away. Tears flowed down his cheeks.

"Can you get a message to my parents?" asked Treetump.

"Of course."

"Tell them to come to the edge of the pool and call for me four times. If I am able, I will come to them. Tell them everything that has happened. Tell them to please not be afraid of me, for I am still their son." Those were the last words he ever spoke.

When Treestump no longer had any human qualities, he turned his head slowly for a final glance at Longbow, then slithered from beneath the blanket and writhed his way to the water. With a silent ripple of the pool's surface, Treestump disappeared.

———

The next morning, Treestump's mother and father came to the pool and called his name four times, as they were told to do. They sat quietly on the water's edge and waited without speaking, for everything that could be said had been said the night before, a long night of grief and tearful sobbing.

In a few minutes, the father pointed to a long black snake swimming toward them. Making his way from the pool, the snake curled up between the two, laying his head on his mother's lap. His father reached to touch him.

"We will always be your parents, son," he said. After a short while, the snake lifted his head in a slight nod and slithered to the water.

For the next two weeks, the parents visited their son every day, and Treestump always came soon after they called. As their visits grew less frequent, the snake would sometimes not appear for half an hour or more after they called for him.

Though he would always occupy their memories, the time came when his parents came to call but once a year. Treestump gradually became less of what he had been and more and more what he had become—a long, thin, and handsome snake.

The Hunters' Wives

In long-ago times, when men left for a hunting trip, they would stay gone for several days, sometimes a week. The elders warned hunters about letting their thoughts drift away from the hunt and on matters of home.

"There is danger in thinking of home while hunting," they said.

Two hunters once traveled a day's distance from their homes and were setting up their campsite when the younger one said, "I am feeling homesick."

"You should not think about home, you know that," said his friend. "Think about yourself, about what you'll catch tomorrow."

When darkness came, they built a fire and were settling in for the night, when they heard movement in the woods. Something was approaching the camp. The two hunters stood, gripping their weapons, for they were expecting no visitors.

"Hello!" came a friendly voice, and the hunters were surprised to see their two wives step into the light of the campfire.

"We have brought food for your supper," said the home-sick man's wife. The men glanced at one another, for the women had apparently carried the food a great distance. The women began preparing the food, and the young hunter helped his wife as she directed him.

"We could use more firewood," she said. "Is this all the water? Maybe you can bring more. The creek is not far away."

The older hunter was still uncertain about what was happening.

My wife, he thought, *would never walk this far to join me on a hunting trip. She knows of the danger. I have been on long hunts before. This is not like her.* The two women looked like the hunters' wives, spoke as they spoke, and in every way appeared to be who they claimed to be.

The old hunter had a dog, very old himself, who was always watchful for the hunter. He sidled up to the old man while the wives were cooking.

"You should tell your friend these women are not your wives," the dog said. "You should not eat with them." The dog seldom spoke, but he had never been wrong in his warnings. He had the power to see through even the strongest magic and evil.

The old hunter followed his friend to the creek and, once they were out of earshot of the camp, told him, "You know my dog watches out for me. He has warned me that we should be careful. The women are not who we think they are. He says we should not eat with them."

"It will be fine if you do not eat with them. I think it is funny that you would believe your dog. You can recognize your own wife," said the young hunter.

"I had my suspicions before the dog spoke," said the older hunter.

"Well," said the younger man, "she is my wife and I am eating with her."

While the younger hunter and the woman who looked like his wife ate, the older man said, "I am not hungry."

The young couple stayed up late talking and finally retired in the shadows on their side of the camp. As the fire burned low, the older hunter's dog nudged him and said, "When the woman who looks like your wife comes to you, pick up a piece of burning firewood and poke her with it." The hunter nodded.

When the second woman stepped around the fire and

came to sit beside him, he grabbed a long stick of burning wood and struck her in the side with it. She immediately screamed, turned into a small fox, and ran away.

"Who was that screaming?" asked the young hunter, leaping to his feet. The older hunter followed the fox a short distance, to be certain it would not return. He then approached his friend, still carrying the burning wood.

"That was the woman who looked like my wife. She turned into a fox and fled when I touched her with this fire-wood. You must do the same. These women are not our wives. They are not even women."

"I did not see a fox, and I don't know why you chased your wife away," said the young hunter. "I am here with my wife, and I am glad she joined us."

The old man stood helplessly and watched his friend return to the strange woman. A sad feeling overcame him.

"There is nothing you can do for him," said the dog. "It is too late."

The old hunter struggled to stay awake, listening for the slightest sound of danger, ready at any moment to leap to help his young friend. Exhausted from the long day's journey, he finally fell asleep after midnight.

He was awakened by a crunching noise coming from the young hunter's camp. It was the sound dogs make as they fight over a common kill, eating quickly before their food is taken. It was the sound of the woman who appeared to be the young hunters' wife, devouring him as he lay sleeping.

"Stay quiet," the dog said. "Let her finish with him. He is already dead. I am trying to save you." The hunter rose quietly and followed the dog, carrying his gun and slinking away from the camp.

"When she finished with him, she planned on making a meal of you as well," said the dog. Several young pups were sleeping on the edge of the camp, and the old dog told them,

"We are going to help our master, just as if we were young men. You all run ahead and find a safe hiding place. Be quick!" The dogs did as they were told, while the two old ones, the dog and the hunter, followed slowly behind.

Soon the young dogs were yelping and dashing back to they old ones, saying, "We've found a cave." Overhead came the piercing scream of an owl's call.

"Hurry!" said the old dog, urging his master to safety. When the old ones reached the cave and scrambled inside, the owl flew down and tried to claw his way past the dogs and into the cave. The hunter crawled to the back of the cave and soon the sound of wild barking and screeching cries filled the dark air. The young dogs and the owl were doing battle. The old dog kept watch at the opening of the cave, in case the owl should try to enter.

The loud cries were soon replaced with the soft whimpering sounds of wounded animals.

"The owl is too tired to fight anymore,' the old dog said. "He is sitting and watching. I think he is trying to find the energy to leave before the young dogs gather their strength again."

When morning came, the owl was gone. The hunter and his dog emerged from the cave and looked carefully about. Two young dogs were cut and bleeding, but not seriously.

When the hunter and his dog returned to the camp, the strange women were still there, sitting peacefully as if nothing had happened. The ways of evil are difficult to explain or understand. The hunter gathered his belongings and left quickly, without speaking to the two.

When the elders speak, it is always best to listen. When you are involved in one journey, when you are hunting, do not to think of the home front. Keep your attention where you are. There are dangers otherwise.

Panther Man

Younger brothers often have a hard time of it. Sometimes they feel left out. Sometimes they are tempted to believe what their older brothers say about them. Katcilutci*, or Little Panther Foot, was a little brother, so he knew well the cloud these feelings bring.

"Catch this," his oldest brother said one day on the river bank, tossing him a heavy bundle of wood and knocking him to the ground—this when he was four years old. The three middle brothers laughed as Katcilutci fell on his back.

"Crybaby," they said, laughing, but Katcilutci refused to cry. Instead, he rose to his feet and struggled to lift the bundle. He inched his little arms beneath it and silenced his brothers as he brought the bundle to his chest.

"Where would you like me to carry it?" he asked.

"Look at you, Little Panther Foot," said the oldest brother, and a new and welcome flame, a flame of admiration, flickered in his eyes. "You can carry it to the house. We'll be here fishing. Just let us know that you've done it."

The others laughed, for the house was over a mile away.

"Don't be so quick to laugh," said the oldest. They watched as Katcilutci carried the bundle as far as he could, falling over twice, before rolling the wood, then dragging the wood, always moving the bundle toward the house however he could.

An hour later Katcilutci returned to his brothers and said, "The wood is at the house. Mother told me to thank you for sending it."

---

*pronounced *kut-che-LO-chee*

Though the taunting and laughter continued as the brothers grew, for that is the fate of the youngest, the others often felt the pride that comes of seeing family members triumph when looking at Katcilutc; Little Panther Foot.

Katcilutci was not the youngest in the family. A beautiful girl came after him. Her brothers often warned her of the dangers she would face when not under their protective shadow.

"You are sweet and innocent," said the oldest.

"You are beautiful, too," said the others.

"You must be careful where you go, who you speak to," the oldest continued.

––––

One summer day a panther, looking much like a man but in truth a Man-Eater, rowed his boat to the river bank where the sister was dipping her feet in the water.

"Step on the boat," he said to the girl. "We can go for a ride, just to the other shore." When the girl said nothing and did not move, he said, "Just a short ride. The boat is safe and sturdy."

The girl cocked her head as if to say, *It is not the boat that concerns me.*

Man-Eater laughed, more interested than ever in the beautiful girl who was bright as well. Pointing to a blanket in the rear of the boat, he told her, "I have four tiny panthers under the blanket. Let me show them to you." The girl stood, looking over her shoulder to the house.

"See them wiggle," he said. "They're cute little things. Come see."

––––

The girl gripped the edge of the boat and eased herself over the side, lifting her hand and refusing his help as she did so. When she lifted the blanket, Man-Eater flung it over her, struck her in the head with a large stone, and pushed the boat away from the shore. He rowed the boat upstream, and when the girl awakened she saw the thick woods on the river bank and knew she was being carried far away from her home.

"Where are you taking me?" she asked.

"To my home," he said. "You will like it there, you will see."

The girl realized that appearing docile and agreeable would give her the best chance to escape, so she said nothing. When the boat landed, he led her to his home, a dilapidated wooden shack set back from the river.

"It was a long, hard trip, and I am hungry," Man-Eater said. He left the girl standing while he took off his boots and settled himself in the house.

"There is a room behind the house," he said. "You will find meat there. Bring me some, then go to the river for acorns. That will make a good meal tonight. Wash the acorns in the river. You can begin cooking when you return."

The girl struggled through the underbrush to the room, and there she found an old woman sitting in a dark corner. As she stood in the light of the doorway, the girl saw that the old woman's skin was raked with crevices and her arms were covered with scars.

"Where did you come from?" the old woman asked.

"I live upstream with my brothers," said the girl. "At least I used to before I stepped on the man's boat this morning. I was foolish to do it, and here I am."

"He is more a panther than a man," said the old woman. "You will see, if you stay. He treats me cruelly. If he cannot find anything to eat, or if he is too lazy to hunt, he cuts a piece of meat from my flesh. Did he tell you to bring meat?"

"Yes."

"Do you see any meat in this room?"

"No, but he said I would find meat here," said the girl.

"I am the meat," the woman said, hanging her head in a sadness as deep as any the girl had ever seen. "He means me."

She lifted her dress to her knees to show the girl the missing flesh.

The girl closed her eyes and wrapped her arms around herself, shivering. Her situation was far worse than she had imagined.

"You must not stay here," the woman continued. "When he finishes eating me, he will start on you, I know he will."

"What can I do?"

"Did he tell you to bring acorns?"

"Yes."

The woman stepped to the doorway and called out in a language the girl did not understand. Soon she heard the croaking of frogs. The woman spoke again in the strange tongue, then turned to the girl and said with a shrug, "You learn many things trying to survive in these woods. Talking to frogs is only one of them. You must escape quickly, today."

"What did you say to the frogs?"

"The Man-Eater will soon ask if you have washed the acorns. I told the frogs to answer for you from the river. They will tell him it will not be long, and they'll make him wait as long as possible, giving you time to run away. Now, go!" she said, pointing north into the woods. "Run! Your life is at stake."

The girl reached out and took the old woman's hands in her own. She looked into her sad, green eyes and said, "Thank you." As the girl fled to the woods, the woman returned to her chair in the dark corner, and there she sat and cried quietly for an hour, remembering the sweetness of a tender touch.

———

Soon the Man-Eater grew impatient. "Are you washing the acorns?" he called out.

"Not yet," replied the frogs. Twice more he called, and twice more the frogs replied, before the Man-Eater rose and went looking for the girl. Thinking he had heard her voice in the river, Man-Eater plunged into the water.

"Little girl, why do you swim away from me?" he sang. Hearing no sound, he soon realized the girl was missing.

Man-Eater had a special wheel, Motarkah, which had its own mind and could find anything or anyone that was lost. Man-Eater threw Motarkah in the direction of the river, but each time he threw it there, Motarkah returned and rolled to a stop at his feet. Finally, he threw Motarkah into the woods. The wheel began rolling at a fast pace, following the trail of the girl, and Man-Eater leapt to the path and joined the pursuit.

The girl heard the sounds of her pursuers crashing through the underbrush. She screamed out, recalling the fate of the old woman and knowing it would be her fate if she were caught.

Her brothers were hunting in the nearby woods, and the youngest brother said, "Listen. Our sister is crying for help."

"You are hearing things," said the others. "We miss her, too, but she is gone."

"No, I heard her voice. Listen!"

The oldest brother held his hand up and said, "Be quiet." In the silence, the brothers clearly heard their sister calling, singing with all her lung power as she ran.

"Brothers!" she cried. "I must reach our house before they catch me. Help me, brothers!" The brothers ran to the sound and from a small hill saw the girl being chased by Man-Eater and Motarkah.

"Stay behind," they said to the youngest. "You are too young to go. Stay behind and cook."

But Little Panther Foot followed after the brothers. When they came to Motarkah, they shot arrows at him, but he was a stout wheel and rolled so fast, they could do nothing to stop him. The girl fled past the brothers, but right on her heels went Motarkah, and not far behind him came Man-Eater.

The youngest brother carried with him the wooden

paddle he used to parch the food for cooking. He saw his brothers stand helplessly as the wheel rolled by, and when he saw Man-Eater, he knew his sister's life was in danger. He let his sister pass, then stood in the pathway of Motarkah. At the last moment, when Motarkah could not change his direction, he jumped aside, striking the wheel with the wide end of the paddle.

Motarkah swerved off the path and came to a halt at the base of a tree. The girl spotted her youngest brother and ran to him, closely followed by Man-Eater. She hid behind her brother as Man-Eater flashed his claws and showed his flesh-eating teeth.

Little Panther Foot stood firm, and when Man-Eater was within range, he swung the paddle with all of his strength, striking the panther man on the back of the head.

Man-Eater fell at their feet. He made one futile attempt to reach for the girl with his outstretched claws before he died.

Their hearts filled with gratitude and respect, the oldest brother and sister took their young brother by the arm and made their way home.

"Pick up the paddle and carry it home," the oldest said to the other brothers, "and see what you can cook for supper tonight. Maybe it is time for someone besides our youngest brother to do the cooking."

"I know someone who would be glad to help with the cooking," said the sister, "as long as she has plenty of help and respect."

The next day the old woman from the thick-wooded river bank joined her new family. Though her life was not perfect, for she still had those selfish middle brothers to contend with, she soon became a deeply happy woman.

The Tie-Snakes

Grandfather Haney saw the boy looking at the mounds of dirt by the river.

"Know what those are, Grandson?"

"No," said the boy.

"They are graves, Grandson. Graves that carry a story from the past and post a warning for the future," old man Haney said. "First you should know the story from the past. It began when a Creek chief entrusted his son with a message for another chief."

————

"I am putting my trust in you, Boney," said the Creek chief, handing his son a vessel containing an important message to another chief. "Do not disappoint me."

"I will see that it is delivered," said Boney. He shouldered the food, blanket, and small hunting gear his mother had packed for him and began the four-day journey.

He had traveled less than a day west of his home when he heard boys laughing in a nearby woods. Boney veered from the path and followed the sound to a wide and slow-flowing river.

"Who are you?" the largest boy asked.

"My name is Boney."

"Where are you from?"

"Not far," Boney replied. The boys studied Boney and decided he was to their liking. The large one picked up a stone and tossed it into the water. Soon all the boys were scrambling for stones and peppering the surface of the water.

They threw larger and larger stones, each trying to outdo

the other, till one of the boys noticed a deep rippling washing from the center of the river to the shore.

"Look," said the cautious one, pointing to the wave. "What is making that wave?"

The other boys paid no attention but continued throwing the stones, dashing about and prying up all the large stones on the river bank. Finding no large stone, Boney picked up the vessel containing his father's message and tossed it in the river.

"Wow!" said the boys. "That made quite a splash. What was it?"

"It belongs to my father," Boney said. The boys looked at each other without speaking.

"No need to worry," said Boney. "I'm sure it will float. Help me spot it when it comes to the surface."

Boney knew the vessel was too heavy to float. He shrank into a fearful knot inside himself, hoping for some way of reversing what he had done. After a few minutes spent studying the water's surface, the large boy said, "Looks like it's gone." The others hung their heads in silence, sensing the seriousness of Boney's dilemma.

———

To Boney's credit, he did not want to lie to his father about how he lost the message. He climbed a cypress tree and crawled out on a sturdy limb hanging over the river.

"Careful," said the cautious boy. "It is not safe in the river. There's something living in the deep waters. Some of the old people say they've seen it swimming, huge and dark. You don't want to fall in this river, not here."

"I have to get the vessel," Boney said. "There is no choice. My father trusted me." Casting a last look at his new friends, he continued, "If I do not come back, please tell my father what happened."

"Where is your father? Where do you live?" they called, but Boney could not hear them. He had already plunged into the river. The boys immediately ran to the spot where he entered the water, for they knew of the dangers. When Boney did not return for half an hour, they reported his death to their parents.

———

Once beneath the water's surface, Boney waved his arms and kicked his legs, turning a complete circle and peering through the clear waters as he searched for the vessel.

It sank to the bottom, he thought, and flipped over in a diving motion, determined to find the vessel. Only a few swimmer strokes from the surface, he felt his arms pinned to his sides. He knew he was struggling for his life, but he was unable to free himself. His lungs were bursting in a painful fire. He closed his eyes and wished he could be with his own people, with his family. He wished he had never taken this trip.

His attackers carried Boney deeper and deeper into the river, till the boy felt himself falling into a swoon. Suddenly, Boney felt the pain slip away. He opened his mouth and was able to breath. When his eyes focused, he saw himself being carried into an enormous underwater cave. Two tie-snakes held his arms, but they loosened their grip in a gesture of friendship.

Boney turned his eyes to the depths of the cave and saw a giant snake staring at him. He appeared to be occupying a large platform, but looking closer, Boney saw that the platform was a mass of slithering and writhing snakes.

"Climb," said the snake. Boney made three attempts, falling each time and feeling the slippery skin of the snakes slide over his own. On the fourth try, he ascended the platform and stood beside the snake.

"Take that feather," the snake said, pointing to a feather in the corner of the platform. The boy tried three times before grasping the feather on the fourth try.

"That tomahawk is yours as well," said the snake, and

Boney saw the sharp weapon sticking through the platform of snakes. Again he retrieved the object on the fourth attempt.

When he once again sat by the King of the Tie-Snakes, the snake said, "You can return to your father in three days. He thinks you are dead, but he will soon forget those feelings in the joy of finding you alive. Do not tell him everything you know, but if you ever are in severe danger, tell him to walk to the east. He then must bow three times, and I will be there to help your people."

Three days later the tie-snakes carried Boney to the surface of the river and handed him his father's vessel. By eveningtime, Boney was reunited with his father, who was overjoyed to see him alive.

"Where have you been?" his father asked.

Boney told of the tie-snakes. "There is more," he said, "but I can only tell you if we are in danger, great danger. Please do not ask me to break my promise to the King of the Tie-Snakes."

"Of course not," said his father. "I am proud of you for keeping your promises."

In only a few weeks, the chief's enemies chose to attack. Their forces were overwhelming and death loomed for the Creeks.

"You understand the tie-snake's promise," the chief told Boney. "It is time to seek his help." Boney instructed his father to travel east and bow three times. In the dark of night, the chief began his walk to the east.

When daybreak came, every enemy soldier was held in the grasp of a snake. The Creek chief made peace with all of his enemies.

———

"So you see, Grandson, the tie-snakes have a special place in the history of the Creek people."

"What is the warning?" asked the boy, looking at the mounds.

"Those mounds come from more recent times, Grandson. A boy heard the story of the tie-snakes and foolishly tried to dive into the waters. He met the snakes, as he wished, but not the friendly snakes of the old story. Instead, he was pulled below the water. He cried for his father, who leapt in the river in a vain attempt to save the boy.

"Both drowned, and both are buried in these mounds. Their graves remain by the river as a reminder of the power of the tie-snake. Respect the old mysterious powers, Grandson, and never tempt them."

Long-Clawed One

Dogs can spot witches. They can recognize a witch in whatever form the witch may choose, whether owl or person, raccoon or other animal, a dog can spot a witch. A smart person knows this and listens to his dog, while the unwise often suffer the horror of turning a deaf ear to the warnings of a faithful friend.

The McIntosh family loved their dog as if he were a member of the family, and they treated him so. When Joneth McIntosh cooked pork or deer meat for supper, she always pulled a leg from the fire with a little bloody meat still sizzling, just the way Buck liked it, and while the family dove into the meat at the evening meal, Buck lay down at the foot of the table, sweeping the wooden floor with his tail and gnawing the meat with old but still-sharp canine teeth.

When visitors came, Buck always greeted them as they entered the yard, sniffing and circling and using whatever means of divination dogs have been granted, determining the friend-or-foe status of the newcomer. Only once did the family choose to ignore Buck's warning, and it cost Buck his life, though he gave it willingly.

One day a small boy entered the clearing at the McIntosh place. He appeared to be only about eight years old and was so thin it looked as if he had not eaten for several days. Long before he came into view, Buck caught the scent of the boy and heard him walking on the dried leaves of the autumn floor. He dashed to meet him, keeping his nose to the ground, sniffing like he was on a hunt and closing in on his prey. When he lifted his eyes and saw the boy, he stood

146

his ground and bared his teeth. The boy changed his path and circled around Buck.

The dog dashed to the front porch and started up with a low growling sound, punctuated by a long, low howl, as dogs will sometimes do at the full moon, joining their cousins the wolf and coyote in a deep and mysterious song that humans will never understand.

Old man McIntosh—Sam to his friends—stepped to the porch, leaned over, and touched Buck on the back of the neck.

"What's the matter, Buck? Settle yourself down, boy."

In a minute the boy came into view, dressed in a ragged blue shirt and dark brown britches that looked handmade. Buck edged himself against Sam, pressing hard against his legs, walking around him but never moving away, growling and baring his teeth at the young boy as he did so.

"What is it?" asked Joneth, Sam's wife, stepping onto the porch. "Oh, my. Look at you," she said, walking to the boy as Buck began to bark. She turned to Sam and said, "Tie him up out back, Sam. No need to make such a racket about a hungry boy."

Sam gripped Buck by the collar and dragged him around the house to a chopping stump in the back yard. He tied a stout rope around his collar and Buck immediately started gnawing the rope. Sam turned to go, but Buck barked at him in a way he had never heard before.

Ruff, ruff, ruff, ruff— four quick yips, followed by a pause and a yelp. Buck repeated this pattern over and over till Sam turned to him, aware for the first time that Buck had a knowledge even deeper than Sam had ever believed.

"What is it, Buck?" he asked, and when he voiced the question, Sam spoke as if he were speaking to a friend of his, a hunting companion.

Urrrr, Buck replied. *Urrr*, he whistled. Sam sensed the effort Buck was making to warn him of the boy. The fur on

Buck's shoulders stood up straight, and when Sam knelt to him and asked again, "What is it?" he saw a resignation in the eyes of his dog, as Buck slumped his shoulders and hung his head.

"What do you know, my friend?" said Sam.

"Know that I will give my life for you," said Buck, and in his eyes Sam saw a terrifying scene. He saw an old man with white-dead skin and sharp claws ripping at his dog, tearing him to pieces, and Buck struggling and fighting to his death.

"No, Buck," he shouted, standing to his feet. "This will not happen." But by the manner of Buck's response and the presence of tears rolling down Buck's face, he knew that Buck spoke an irrefutable truth. He untied the rope binding him and said, "Give me time to get Joneth back in the house, then get after the stranger best you can. I'll get my gun and join you."

Sam walked a brisk step to the front porch while Buck crept around the side of the house, readying himself to pounce on the young boy as soon as Joneth was safely inside.

The boy was sitting on the top porch step as Joneth stooped to hand him a full plate of food. Sam took her by the elbow so brusquely, leading her through the door, she almost dropped the food in the boy's lap.

"What are you doing?" Joneth said. "That boy is our guest!"

"You have to believe what I am telling you," said Sam. "We are feeding a witch. Stay in the house."

Joneth lightly pulled her arm away, then her eyes were drawn to a struggle taking place on the porch. Buck was growling like a rabid dog and tearing at the boy's sleeve. When the boy stood and slapped at Buck, drawing a deep cut from his mouth to his ear and sending a curling arc of dark blood across the green of the yard, Joneth stopped her struggles and clung to her husband.

"Do something, Sam," she said. Sam turned to get his shotgun as she said, "Hurry!"

By the time he returned with his weapon, the boy was now the man Sam had seen in Buck's eyes. His sickly, pale skin sagged from his face in clumps, and long, thin claws grew from his fingertips like slivers of razorblades. Sam shouldered his gun and fired a quick round. The sound of the blast sent the old man reeling from the porch and fleeing into the nearby woods.

"Come here, Buck," Sam called, but he knew as he said it his dog would not relax till Buck or the witch was dead. He tucked his gun under his arm and followed a barking and howling Buck into the woods.

Sam trailed the sound of his dog for less than half a mile into the pines when a heavy, ominous silence fell over the trees and underbrush, blanketing the green foliage and red bark of the pines with a palpable, breathing fear. He paused and knelt to the ground, circling the woods with a quiet and seeing gaze.

A hundred yards ahead, Sam spotted Buck lying motionless in a thick tangle of brush. He sprinted to him, and as he drew near Buck struggled to lift his head. Blood ran freely from a series of cuts running the length of his ribs. Sam set his shotgun against a tree and crouched to Buck, but the dog suddenly bared his teeth and leapt past his master.

The old man had slipped behind Sam. He swatted the gun and sent it flying into the trees, then turned his attention to the attacking dog. He flung an arm at Buck, slicing the skin of his neck and shoulders. Buck was soon soaked in red, shaking his head to clear the blood from his eyes.

He is already half-dead, struggling to save my life, not his own, thought Sam.

Buck ran headlong into a clearing with Sam close behind. A hollow log lay on the edge of the trees, and Buck uttered his last bark urging his master to climb into the log.

Sam dove into the narrow opening and rolled his body into a position that allowed him to see through the entryway.

Sam watched with growing sadness and deep pride as his dog flung himself at the Long-Clawed One, time after time, and each attack resulted in a new wound. With one front leg dangling by a thin strand of severed muscle, Buck seemed to summon his remaining strength. He leapt at the neck of the Long-Clawed One, sending him stumbling into the woods and clutching his throat with both hands.

———

No one ever found the body of the Long-Clawed One, but Sam and Joneth were never again bothered by evil intruders. Buck was buried in a place of honor in a cluster of family gravehouses. For many years following his death, the McIntosh household was protected by six fine and eager hunting dogs, Buck's progeny, who surrounded the house with canine loyalty and familial love. If you have a dog, you know the power of this love. It is sweet and everlasting.

Seminole Stories

Nearly 10,000 modern Seminoles, most living in Oklahoma, trace their heritage to settlements established in Florida in the early 1800s. Before that time, the Seminoles were not a single tribal people. Oncoming Anglo settlers pushed remnants of the Alabama and Georgia Creeks—and several other scattered tribes—into Florida, where they were joined by escaping slaves. These determined people, Indians and African-Americans, banded together to form the Seminole Nation. The word Seminole is believed to be derived from the Spanish word cimarron, meaning "wild" or "runaway," possibly because of the large number of runaway slaves that were adopted into the nation.

During the late 1830s, when the Seminoles resisted removal to Indian Territory, the U.S. Army began a series of undeclared wars against them. The army was intent on eliminating this safe haven for runaway slaves, but the fighting conditions were unlike any seen in previous wars. Disease and suicide took high tolls among soldiers. The Seminole Wars lasted for several years, finally resulting in the capture and forced removal of several thousand Seminoles to Oklahoma. In an all-too familiar pattern, many Seminoles died en route to the new homeland.

When the United States finally called a halt to the fighting, around three hundred remaining Seminoles disappeared once again into the swamps. Surrounded by mystery, these swampland people lived in a world of striking beauty—beauty that could kill with a single step, or misstep, in the murky world of half-water, half-earth of the present-day Florida Everglades.

The Seminoles were a people in a state of constant upheaval, pursued first by settlers and later by soldiers. Characteristic of a people on the move, funeral grounds for traditional Florida Seminoles were often randomly selected clearings in the swamps. Cooking utensils, clothing, and household items belonging to the deceased were left near the unburied body. Following careful rituals designed to prevent the dead from returning to life, the living left the dead alone, hoping the dead would return the favor. In the story, "Hungry for Meat," disturbing a gravesite does indeed awaken the dead.

In the Seminole world view, spirits are considered neither supernatural nor otherworldly, but are instead active participants in this world, the natural world. Seminoles were, and are, constantly on guard against conjurers of evil medicine. Conjurers live in secrecy among the people, like the shape-shifting owl-man searching for his young bride in "Chichibow" and the apprenticing witch Pushing Boy from "Yerby's Apple Doll"—a story based on the still-popular craft of apple carving.

As in the old days, modern Seminole witches often take on other forms, such as owls, dogs, or bears, watching and ensnaring their prey. This ability makes witches especially dangerous and fearful, and a cloud of suspicion hovers over every stranger, human or animal. A bird flying overhead or a snake slithering across a log could be a witch, silently following and waiting for a moment of weakness.

Modern Seminoles, predominately Christian, pay homage to the traditional world of tribal medicine and lore. Corn Lady is still honored as a benevolent woman—some say a witch—who sacrificed her life to give the people corn, while Old Twisted Horn is a taker of people's lives before their time.

In 1957, the official Seminole Tribe of Florida received federal recognition. The modern capital of the Seminole Nation of Oklahoma is Wewoka, southeast of Oklahoma City. With a strong foot in both the western and the Indian worlds, the Seminole people straddle a fascinating fence of cultures, heeding the warnings of the old stories as they tread a careful path through the swamps and confusions of everyday life.

Old Twisted Horn

Talago always said, "My husband Lester can sleep through anything. He sleeps as hard as he works." Everybody knew Lester was a hard worker, so when he fell asleep around mid-afternoon at the stomp dance, off in a clump of possum-haw hollies, nobody thought anything about it. When Talago's best friend Etta Mae brought him a plate of food just after dark and couldn't wake him up, folks just smiled and let him sleep.

"I 'magine he needs the rest," somebody said.

"Every one of us is getting old," said somebody else.

When breakfast came the next morning and the music quieted down, Talago stood over him with her arms folded and a worried look creased her brow.

"He's not even snoring," she announced. "Something is wrong."

"He is lying in the same position I saw him in last night," said Etta Mae. "He hasn't even moved."

Folks stood and talked in small groups of close family and friends for a short while, till Old Man Buster said, "We better send a runner to see what the Medicine Man says about all this." A good Medicine Man lived a half-day's walk away and the fastest runner was sent to tell him about Lester and seek his advice.

———

In half the time it would take a young person walking to reach the Medicine Man, the runner returned.

"He says Twisted Horn has stolen Lester's heart," he told Talago and the others. "If we don't get his heart back in four days, Lester will die."

"Where does Twisted Horn live?" asked Talago.

"Medicine Man says he lives way up in the sky, higher than anybody could ever climb."

"What does he say we do?"

"He didn't say. Only that we have four days, no more, then Lester's dead."

"Can we send a bird?" asked Talago.

"Medicine Man says a bird can't fly that high," said the runner.

The gathered dancers hung their heads and left Talago to her thoughts. Soon the dancing started again. Turtle shells ratt-tatt-tattled and high-pitched voices cut the air, urging good medicine, appealing for old Lester.

From beneath the shaking ground Talago thought she heard small voices. She nestled her thumbs behind her ears and cupped her palms around her head. The voices were speaking to her, she was sure of it.

"We can go," said the voices. "We can get his heart for you."

"Listen!" yelled Talago. "Listen to the voices."

Talago's friends ran to her side. "Here, you should sit down and rest," they said, leading her away from the dancing.

"Do you hear voices?" they asked each other. Everyone shook their heads, saddened to see Talago lose her husband and her senses both.

The next day Lester lay still as deadwood and Talago barely moved from his side.

"His face is growing paler by the hour," said Old Man Buster.

"The voices are real," muttered Talago, but she knew no one believed her. "They say they can save Lester."

——

When the morning of the third day arrived, Talago was

seen wandering in the woods around the stomp grounds, upturning logs of every size and crawling under bushes.

"She is looking for the voices," they said.

Near dark, with only the short part of a day to go, two mice jumped onto Talago's lap. "We can get Lester's heart," they said in unison.

"You two have been trying to get my attention," said Talago. The mice nodded. "What makes you think you can get to Twisted Horn?"

The mice only looked at one another without speaking.

"I have to believe in something," said Talago, smiling a wistful smile and reaching for the hopeful mice, who jumped onto her outstretched palm. "Go get my Lester's heart, little friends," she said. "Bring my husband back to me!"

———

That night Talago slept in the woods, under a canopy of sycamores. As she lay on her back, looking at a black sky drooping heavy with stars, she saw a large spider weaving her web across the darkness. She squinted her eyes and peered beyond the spider, trying to see the end of the spider web. The spider appeared to be weaving her web across the sky itself; the web was dangling from thin air.

"Strange wonders are walking tonight," Talago said to herself.

As the spider web crisscrossed the sky, its lines and angles shimmered silvery in the moonlight. Talago spotted the two mice, carefully climbing the web, higher and higher, till she could see them no longer. For the first time in days, she fell asleep in the warm blanket of hope.

———

The mice reached the place where Twisted Horn lived after midnight. They scurried about his room, unafraid of making noise, more concerned with finding where he kept the hearts he had stolen. In a corner they found a wooden box and saw blood dripping through the cracks.

"There it is," said one, and the mice dashed to the red-streaked box.

"The smell of blood is strong," said the other. The mice began to gnaw on the leather lock. Twisted Horn heard the racket, rolling over in his laziness.

"Who is that?" he asked. The mice said nothing, just went about their work. When the lock was cut, they squeezed inside the box. There they found hearts of the long-dead, hearts of the soon-to-be-dead, and hearts of many who still lived, unaware that their days were numbered.

The mice found the still-beating heart of Lester. The blood was dark red and still warm.

"Lester can live if we hurry," they said. As they fled out the door and jumped on the spider web, they turned to scold Twisted Horn.

"You are evil," said one. "You prey on the good and hard-working people."

"You will always be alone," said the other.

——

As morning came, Talago was surrounded by friends who gathered close around her and watched the red streaks of dawn climb higher in the sky. "Daylight this morning without a heart means death to Lester," whispered Etta Mae. "See how the sky bleeds."

"Yes," said Talago. "The sky is bleeding. It is Lester's blood! The mice are returning with his heart!"

The dancers turned their eyes to the sky and beheld the holy sight. The two tiny mice were racing with all their speed down the spider web. Five feet from the ground, as the first yellow sliver of dawn flashed from the mountaintop to the gathered ones, the mice jumped onto Lester's chest and pushed his heart into the cavity, filling the emptiness.

Lester sat up and said, "That was maybe the best sleep I ever had." When everybody laughed and cheered, he stared and wondered why.

———

While people stood and pondered what to do, the mice had risked their lives. "From now on," Talago declared, "the mice are welcome to eat the corn hearts. No people should ever deny them their reward."

No one argued with Talago. From that day to this one, mice are welcome to eat the Seminole corn; and for the rest of her days, if Talago wanted to talk to strange voices, no one said a word.

Hungry for Meat

People bury the dead in all different kinds of ways. Some people bury the dead in bone bundles, in barely noticeable dirt mounds near their homes. Others build grave houses, actually little more than a roof on top of the ground, and they place the body of the deceased under the roof, surrounded by earthen walls. At one end of the gravehouse is a door, for the spirit to come and go as it pleases. Spirits like to come and go as they please, you know?

Some people are so afraid of the dead, and the whole idea of death, that they bury the dead in unmarked graves, and never utter the person's name again, for fear that it might bring them back from the dead. Many people bury their dead all in one place, in graveyards, sometimes behind churches, sometimes in trees on the edge of town. Some like to know where the dead are, to visit and speak to them, to lay special things, flowers or flags, on the gravesite.

But that's not true of everybody. Seminole people used to bury their dead in random places, sometimes in the swamps where the smells are thick and stagnant and the moss hangs low, like the hair of the dead. A person not paying attention might stumble on a grave in the woods and not even notice, for a gravesite might first appear as a campsite, with things that belonged to the person scattered about, dishes, furniture, clothing.

Dead people won't do you any harm, at least not usually. If you stay away from their home, they'll stay away from yours. The problem comes when people disturb graves without even knowing it. If one morning you crawled out of bed to find a total stranger cooking in your kitchen, you'd want to run him out of your house. Why would spirits of the dead be any different?

———

A young Seminole hunter once poled his boat to the opposite shore of the Chattahoochee River, to a place he'd never been before. He gathered his gear and found a rotten log to hide the boat behind, scattering leaves and branches over it. He had heard of a thick clump of trees not far from the shore where the deer and game were plentiful, and he turned his sights in that direction.

As he moved away from the river and into the swamp, walking was slow on the black mud, for the ground seemed to suck his every step deep into itself, only releasing his feet with a loud, reluctant *squish!* Swarms of mosquitoes hummed and sang about his ears, and the leaves dripped with moisture.

The hunter was moving to the west, in the direction of the setting sun, but the trees blocked out the sky and he was so intent on hacking his way through the vines, night was on him before he knew it. He should have stopped. The grass was up to his knees and he couldn't see his own feet, but on he went, lured into the swamp by the moonlight filtering thin and fragile through the trees.

As he neared the hunting grounds, he stumbled on a clearing. He moved to the center and waited for his eyes to adjust to the light, blue and hazy in the thick fog. For a quarter of an hour he stood, unmoving and surrounded by the loud humming and swift calls of the swamp. When his eyes cleared, he saw elements of human life: bowls and household items, pieces of beaded clothing, even a pair of shoes.

He looked for a fire to feel the ashes, for it's always good to know, especially in the swamp, if you are truly alone or if you have strangers for company. He found no fire and thought it curious. He picked up a bowl and held it up to the moonlight. Seeing only a few dead ants in the bottom and no sign of use in recent days, he set it aside and left the camp.

As he entered the clump of trees, he heard a rustling in the leaves. He turned and saw the shadow of a fleeing doe. He watched her flit and dash among the brush, moving away from him and onto a small rise above the floor of the swamp. He knew he could never outrun her in the dark, so he followed her to the knoll and found a comfortable perch on a fallen log to wait, in case she might retrace her steps and dart his way. Soon she did, stepping out of the shadows and into full view. He readied his bow, and the round yellow moon gave a clean view and easy shot. He whispered a prayer and released the arrow, and as the bowstring vibrated and hummed he seemed to feel the arrow slide into the deer's heart.

Not far from where the doe lay dying, the hunter set up his own camp. He built a fire, first with green wood to drive the mosquitoes away with the smoke, then with oak for cooking. Exhausted by the long day's journey, he went about the task of gutting the doe and preparing her for roasting. He hung the deer from a thick tree branch for easy cutting.

On a grill of stones he cooked the meat, to the sizzling sounds and blood-ripe smells of hunter's campsites everywhere.

Some for eating now and some for later, he thought. While he was happy to have the food, the doe was too small for him to call it a successful hunt. The hunter made plans to stay another day, or maybe two, till he could catch a buck. He could eat the doe while looking for a buck to carry home.

With his belly full, the hunter made himself a soft bed by spreading dry leaves on the ground. He pulled a blanket over himself and curled into the ready hope of sleep.

"Meat. Hungry for meat."

At first he thought he dreamed the words. He dreamed

someone had entered his camp, a young woman with hard skin and skinny outstretched fingers. She was pretty, or once had been, but now her hair held cobwebs, and dried mud and leaves clung to her dress.

He woke up, startled by the sound in his ear, close enough for him to feel the breath that bore it.

"Meat. Hungry for meat."

The voice was old and the words seemed more hissed than spoken, as if arising from the mouth of a slumbering beast. He jumped up quickly and turned to see the woman of his dream standing before him.

"I am sorry," he stammered, then looked at her and asked himself, *Why am I apologizing to her? She is the one who crept up on a sleeping man and bent to whisper words into my ear.* He knew he should be angry, but he was not.

"I didn't hear you coming. I was asleep," he said. "You are hungry, you say. I have deer meat. I cooked and killed a doe. Let me get some for you."

As if she hadn't heard his words, she reached out and ran her bony fingers down his neck. They were cold and dry, like jagged, gritty sand. The hunter stepped back, and she groped at him as if she were blind.

"Meat. Hungry for meat," she repeated. He took her by the elbow and led her to the fire. He pulled strips of deep-red meat from the doe's thigh and handed them to the woman. She chewed like a madwoman with no care for appearances, ripping the flesh with the growl of a small dog and ignoring the juice as it drizzled down her cheek and onto her dress.

When she finished the meat, he gave her more, and when she was satisfied she leaned back without speaking. He wrapped a bundle of extra meat and set it on her lap.

"This is for you," he said. "For later." She gave no response, and when he looked into her eyes, they seemed to be glazed, as if she were seeing the world from a far distant place and only now, gradually, was he beginning to come into her view. Her mouth turned upward with the whisper of a smile. She nodded her head in gratitude and said words that made him wonder.

"I should have fed you when you came, but it was too close to daylight."

Shrugging off her words, attributing them to madness, he helped her to her feet.

"Do you know where you are going?" Without speaking, she turned to the river and entered the shadows. The hunter slept a fitful sleep. He dreamed the woman returned, rubbing her dry and calloused fingers on his neck. "Meat. Hungry for meat," she said.

He floated in and out of sleep, always returning to the woman. Just before sunrise he dreamed she sank her teeth into his ear, pulling the flesh away and whispering as she chewed. "Meat. Hungry for meat."

He sat up, wide-awake. He slapped his ear and felt a squirt of warm blood. It was his own, popped from the bellies of four fat mosquitoes who'd been feasting there.

The hunter rose at daylight and, after a quick meal, gathered himself for the hunt, forgetting about his night visitor. Not long before sundown, he found the tracks he was looking for. He could tell by the distance of the front legs to the back, and the depth of the prints in the mud, this was a sizable buck. Though the tracks were fresh, he soon lost the trail. With the sun going down, he returned to his campsite, empty-handed but encouraged at the prospects for tomorrow.

As he stepped into the clearing, he caught the smell of herbs, more musky than sweet. Tilting his head back, he took a breath through his nostrils.

She has been here, he thought. *That is her smell, from the leather pouch she wore around her neck.*

He quickly knelt and dug up the cache of meat he'd buried from the day before.

If she was here, she's taken nothing, he thought, looking about the camp. The hunter pulled dried corn from another pouch and set water on to boil. He took a deer leg from the pouch and set it on a stone, to heat it while he cooked the soup. As the warming meat dripped blood into the fire, he heard footsteps shuffling on dried leaves, just on the edge of darkness.

The hunter stood and turned to the sound, waiting for the woman. The sound ceased, but the woman did not appear. He sat again and waited. From the opposite side of the fire circle, he again heard her steps.

"I have meat for you," he called to the shadows, surprising himself.

For half an hour he heard the sounds, the crackling of dried leaves underfoot. Though he continued to call out, she never came into the clearing. As he felt himself falling asleep, he saw a sliver of white emerging from the dark, arm high. His head slumped over and the vision came full force.

The five fingers of her hand came at the meat, disconnected from her arm and body. They grabbed the leg and lifted it to an unseen mouth. The hunter heard the sound of chewing, and blood fell from the doe's leg.

He jerked awake and lay panting. The meat had fallen into the fire, and it sizzled and shrank in the flickering light. The smell of burning meat was joined by that of musky herbs, floating over the fire and circling his head. The hunter sat up, gathered the blanket around himself, and resolved to stay awake till sunrise.

The stars were flashing quiet blue fire on the deepest dark of night, with only a quarter-hour remaining before dawn. As the hunter sat in the depths of sleep, exhausted from the long night of unseen spirits walking, his most terrifying dream emerged.

The young woman sat before him.

"Meat. Hungry for meat," she whispered, lifting his hand to her lips. Through the cloud of sleep came a flash of pain.

The hunter opened his eyes.

The woman sat before him, as in his dream. She held his hand, as in his dream. Unlike his dream, blood gushed from his fingers. He jerked his hand away, and it was then he saw that half of his thumb was missing.

"Help!" he howled. She smiled, and as she did so, the remainder of his thumb fell from between her teeth.

"Meat. Hungry for meat," she said.

The hunter fell into a swoom. When he awakened, the sun was high and flies covered his hand. The blood had slowed to a trickle. He tore his shirt and wrapped it around the stub.

On his way to the boat, the hunter passed the clearing as before. In the full light of day, he saw something he had missed two days earlier. A woman's skeleton was lying in the shade of a cypress tree. The skeleton was old and brittle, and many of the bones were missing. He started to go, but something stopped him.

The strong and pungent smell of herbs, dried herbs, rose from the skull of the woman. *It is her*, he thought. *She has been dead for years*.

The hunter moved closer and saw something small and black crawling across her face, following the curve of her chin. He leaned to within two feet of her, and his eyes focused on a large fly. Another appeared, then another, walking their halting walk on tiny, stilted legs and emerging from the openings of her skull, the holes of her nostrils and ears, till dozens of them, all at once, raced like an army across her now-quivering jawbone where her lips once hung—her mouth was covered by the flies. He knelt and brushed them away. Fresh blood trickled from her bleached white mouth.

It is my blood, he thought, shaking his head in disgust. His body shivered, and his chest heaved in short, hot breaths. The stub of his thumb throbbed in pain. As the hunter watched with disbelieving eyes, the skin returned to the woman's lips and slowly covered her face, thin and transparent at first, then soft and pink, as it must have been when she was young and very much alive.

A crack of thunder saved his life. He looked to the darkening sky and saw black clouds, filled with rain, and knew he would soon be trapped in the swamp. He leapt to his feet and fled in the direction of his boat. Over his shoulder he heard her calling. Her shrieks filled the crackling air, but the hunter never looked back.

"Meat, hungry for meat," she called.

Yerby's Apple Doll

Yerby loved her apple doll. She was seven years old when she received it. She remembered wrapping her tiny fingers around it and lifting it to her face. She remembered closing her eyes and mouth and drawing in the smells of the apple doll, the cidery smells of rich, brown earth. She placed the doll on a small wooden shelf in the corner of her room. The shelf stood only eighteen inches off the floor, just right for a little girl. Forever after, whenever she picked up her apple doll, she felt like a little girl, washed in apple-blossom memories.

Her neighbors, Virgie and Walter Redwater, made the doll and gave it to Yerby, just to be nice, when they saw her walking by their house crying one day.

A big boy was taking the same shortcut through the woods as Yerby, and when she stooped to pick up a turquoise stone, he stumbled over her. His friends laughed at him, so he pushed her in the bushes and yelled at her.

"Get out of the way!"

Yerby waited for the boys to leave, then rubbed the scratches on her arms and legs and picked herself up for the short walk home. Walter saw her passing in front of his house. He turned to Virgie, saying, "Is Yerby crying?"

"I think so," said Virgie. "Call her over and I'll get her one of the girls' old toys."

"Yerby," called Walter. "Come on over a minute. We got something for you."

Yerby stopped crying the moment she saw the apple doll. With her tiny fists she wiped the tears from her cheeks and said, "Thank you."

Walter patted her on the shoulder, and Virgie made a funny smile and kissed her on the nose. Yerby made the same funny face back at her and, in the bright laughter that followed, she forgot all about the mean boy, the Pushing Boy.

As she turned to go, she remembered the stone. She opened her palm and tugged Virgie's sleeve. "For you," she said. Virgie took the light blue stone and held it like a treasure.

"You don't see many stones like this around here," Virgie said. "Thank you, my sweet little girl."

———

Yerby lived with her mother and father, two sisters and three brothers, in a three-room house in Seminole, Indian Territory. Yerby's grandparents had made the trip from Florida as children, seventy years before. They lived in a small house with a bedroom, a kitchen, and a rear porch with a woodburning stove that served as a gathering place. Their house was a half-mile in the woods behind Yerby's, and her grandparents seldom left their house, mostly to visit their kinfolks, if at all.

Yerby's grandfather knew some of the old medicine ways, but if someone he knew was seriously ill or needed help for other reasons, he would call on more powerful friends from Florida. It was said, though never by Yerby's grandfather, that these men from Florida could start out walking to Oklahoma, and by thinking strong on where they were going they would be there in two hours—not by walking fast or flying or changing into anything, just by thinking strong and going-going to their destination.

When anyone asked him about it, Grandfather always said, "Going where you are going is always the best way." Young people sometimes laughed at this logic, but the older ones, and those that loved them and their ways, including Yerby, they would only nod.

Pushing Boy was very different from Yerby, different from Yerby's people, different from Virgie and Walter. He grew up with people from the woods. His grandmother knew the plants to cure and make things happen, the root tea cures; she knew other ways, like the power of smoke from a burning hornet's nest. She healed the rashes and the coughs and was respected for her gifts.

Pushing Boy's uncles gathered in the woods and sang all night, smoking and chanting till they were more than uncles sitting in the woods. Pushing Boy sat with them sometimes, singing the songs.

One night he saw one uncle pick up a hot coal from the fire and put it in his mouth, rolling his head around. When he spit, a burning squirrel came from his mouth, dashing up a nearby tree before bursting into flames and disappearing in a puff of smoke. Pushing Boy's eyes grew wide.

Pushing Boy sometimes followed the uncle, thinking his uncle never knew. One night he watched as his uncle stood in the back yard of a neighbor he had had a fight with. The uncle sang a special song, over and over, till everyone in the house was so sound asleep they would never wake up without the uncle's help.

Pushing Boy crouched in the shadows and watched as the uncle walked in the back door, going from room to room and filling his pockets with jewelry and special items of the family. Though he never saw the uncle leave the house, Pushing Boy heard the swishing of wings and the call of an owl a few feet over his head. He was startled and fell to the ground, clutching the roots of a red oak tree and cowering from fear.

Soon the uncle stood in the back yard, yelling and waking the family from their deep and dangerous sleep.

From that day, whenever Pushing Boy heard of this uncle fighting or complaining about someone, he followed him that night as he crept away from the singing in the woods, followed him to the home of his enemy, and watched as the uncle chanted everyone to sleep and took whatever he wished from their home.

———

As the years passed and Yerby grew into a teenager, Pushing Boy kept his eyes on her. He grew as well. His bullying nature grew into a vengeful spirit that attached itself to Yerby. He made sure that if she left the house after dark, some unseen noise or wind—an owl call or maybe a chilly breeze in the summer—would torment her.

Then one day Pushing Boy came calling. Yerby's grandmother spotted him first, and though she didn't know who he was, she knew he was up to no good.

"I knew he wasn't the little black dog he appeared to be," she later said.

From her cedar plank bench in her side yard, she saw a dog she'd never seen before, snooping around the windows of Yerby's house, scratching his paws on the windowsills, lifting himself up, turning his head back and forth, real shifty looking.

"He wasn't sniffing the air, like a dog does. In fact," she said, "he must not of smelled like a dog at all, else old Yellow Nose would've got after him quick. That whole litter Yellow Nose come from was fed bee larvae when they was young pups. They *good* watchdogs."

"That black dog we now know was Pushing Boy was looking to see which room the children slept in, to avoid the boys and bother the girls. I wanted to throw a rock, to scare him away. But I thought maybe it be best if he don't know he'd been seen.

"The windows to the boys room musta been open, 'cause I saw him jump right through it. I got up to go get your grandfather, but that black dog, he jumped right back out. Guess he saw how tough them boys is."

As soon as the black dog left the boy's room, he scampered to the woods, and just before he entered the trees, Grandmother saw who it was—Pushing Boy. She called the family together, knowing he would return that evening.

"Maybe we better call for some help," said Grandfather. "If we do it now, they might get here before nightfall."

"Probably best we smoke all 'round the house," said Grandmother, "especially outside the windows where I saw him."

"Why do you think he's after us?" asked Yerby.

"Somebody has made an enemy," said Grandfather.

"Don't take too much to make an enemy these days," said Grandmother, seeing the children slip each other guilty looks. "Just being who you are is enough for some people."

While the elders went about their tasks of smoking and calling, Yerby's mother cracked the corn and put the Pashofa on a slow boil. A medicine man from Florida arrived at Yerby's house just after sundown. He wore a single owl feather in the rattlesnake band of his black hat. Without greeting anyone, he circled the yard, stopping where Pushing Boy had been, spending a long time by the boys' window, before he entered the house.

"He'll be coming back this evening," he said, then looked at Yerby's mother and father and walked out the back door. They joined him on the porch and he told them in a lowered voice, "That Yerby girl needs protecting. Don't say nothing to her, but see she stays in the room with her sisters this evening. Don't let her go outside, no matter what happens."

"Will he hurt her?" Yerby's mother asked.

"Probably try to," said the medicine man.

Virgie and Walter came over for supper that night, carrying blankets. As close-by neighbors, they would be walkers on the same twisting, knotty path as Yerby's family. Virgie smiled to see how pretty Yerby had become. She squeezed

Walter's hand, caught his eye, and moved his glance to Yerby. Walter's eyes beamed to see Yerby's bright, friendly face.

"She doesn't know how pretty she is," he said to Virgie. He thought a minute, then added, "Neither do you. You pretty, too, you know."

Virgie pinched him in the ribs, and the laughter spread warm and full throughout his chest.

"Do you still have the apple doll?" asked Virgie.

"Yes," said Yerby. "It still sits on the shelf in my room."

"You remember that day? How you came by crying and left with the apple doll?"

"You sure made a crying girl happy," said Yerby.

"You know why we gave you that doll?"

Yerby tilted her head in a squinty-eyed question. "Why?"

Virgie held the young girl close, hugged her close, and whispered, "'Cause we love you, Yerby. Keep that love, all of it, close by tonight. Nothing cracks sweet love."

———

Sometime before midnight, Pushing Boy returned. He started his song in the red oaks facing Yerby's window, a deep-voice singing that hid itself in the shadowy rhythms of the night, slipping below the cicadas and joining the moaning of the wind in the pine trees. Soon everyone in the house was sleeping, deadwood logs on a dark and dreamless river.

Pushing Boy walked in the back door without any effort at stealth, as a man would enter his own home. He felt his way along the walls, making his way to Yerby's room. As he stepped to the window to pull back the curtains, his boot knocked over the shelf holding the apple doll. He stooped to pick up the doll, and at the moment his fingers touched the dry skin of the apple, he froze, knowing he was joined in the house by a power far greater than himself.

The faint shifting of a turtle shell rattle sounded—

shoooka—shook—shooka—shook

—shattering the sleeping silence. The dry rattling continued—

shoooka—shook—shooka—shook
shoooka—shook—shooka—shook

—and was soon followed by the high-pitched song of the medicine man. The entire household, the floors and walls and people, seemed to breathe and live again.

Pushing Boy leapt out the window and fled across the yard and into the red oak woods, leaving the singing and rattling far behind him, or so he thought. Another rattling awaited him amongst the trees.

———

"It would be nice," Grandmother later said, "if everybody could just get along. But you have to expect bad things to come to a boy who lived his life that way, stealing from others, roaming around their houses at night. Pushing Boy kept rattling trouble's cage, and it finally just up and bit him."

———

The medicine man was sitting on the back porch, and when he heard hollering coming from the woods, he took his hat off. In a few minutes, a long, thin rattlesnake slithered out of the red oak woods and crawled to the back porch, weaving and twisting his diamondback muscles and climbing one step at a time. He lifted his head to the medicine man and rattled his tail one last time before circling the hat.

The medicine man stuck the owl feather in his rattlesnake hatband and two hours later climbed into his own bed, tired from the long trip but never losing sight of where he was going.

Chichibow

Chichibow always thought that if she moved far enough away, Hadjo would leave her alone. As events unfolded, she realized the exact opposite was closer to the truth. As the miles between them increased, so did the ferocity of his attacks.

———

Unlike the salty chatter and juicy gossip that spiced their cooking conversations, Chichibow and Winnie always leaned closer and talked in hushed tones of secret matters while they shucked corn; but this day's talk carried the eerie feel of destiny. Chichibow held the breath of the matter for as long as she could before posing the question and unleashing the flow to its inevitable conclusion.

"How can my father be so blind?" Chichibow asked. "Even if he were my age instead of so much older than me, he is no good."

Winnie was her best friend, so she offered a respectful pause before she answered, "Maybe you misunderstand."

"What do you mean?"

"Maybe he is your father's friend. Maybe you only think he wants to marry you."

"Winnie, you don't misunderstand something like that," said Chichibow. "My father asked me to be nice to him and make sure his plate stayed full at dinner."

"Sounds like a sure sign to me, that part about the full plate."

"After he left, my mother told me she thought he was nice," said Chichibow, "like she wanted me to agree with her."

"You are right," said Winnie. "Sounds serious to me."

"What can I do if my father wants me to marry him?"

"How much do you love your family?" asked Winnie.

"What do you mean how much do I love my family? They are my family. Of course I love them."

"I didn't ask *if* you loved them. I asked *how much* do you love them."

"What are you thinking?" asked Chichibow.

"Do you love them enough to marry Hadjo to stay close to them?"

"Never. I will never marry him."

"Then that is your answer. You know what you must do."

"Leave my family?" asked Chichibow.

"Leave this place. Leave and go so far way he will never find you."

The two friends slowly stood to straighten their tiring backbones, Chichibow brushing aside a wayward length of hair that fell across her mouth and Winnie wiping sweat from her eyebrows. They both knew that no talk ever held such serious consequences as this one about Hadjo and his misguided affections.

"Tell me if you hear any talk about Hadjo and me," said Chichibow. "Promise me you'll do that."

"Of course," said Winnie. "But you don't need me to tell you anything."

"Why not?"

"Any talk about you and Hadjo will take place in your house. Just keep an eye out for pale gray horses. Hadjo has three of them."

———

The next afternoon, as Chichibow stooped to lift a grapevine loaded with ripe scuppernongs from a fallen log, she spotted a rider approaching her home. She barely lifted her eyes; her father had hundreds of kin and almost as many friends, and he entertained several visitors a week. When she caught the flicker of a gray horse passing through the palmetto bushes, she dropped the vine and shielded her eyes. The shadowy green and yellow spikes cut across the figure of a tall, thin man, hovering low and talking to his horse as he rode.

"Hadjo," she muttered. She tied the bottom of the apron around her waist, securing the grapes from bouncing out of her pockets while she ran, and took off in a dash to the house.

As Hadjo slowed his horse to a canter, Chichibow entered through the back door, grateful that no one saw her. She slipped quietly into her room and crouched by the family-room wall, wrapping a quilt around herself to deaden the sound of any movements she might make.

"Good to see you," she heard her father say, approaching Hadjo as he tied his horse to the front-porch rail. Hadjo only nodded, and Chichibow thought, *He looks down on my father. He thinks he is better than us.*

"Come inside," said Chichibow's father. Chichibow listened as her father stepped to the rear of the house and returned with cooked corn and strips of dried meat.

"Thank you for coming," he said, spreading the meat and corn before Hadjo.

My father wants to please him! Chichibow thought.

Chichibow was grateful she had dragged the quilt from the bed to her corner and wrapped herself in it. She was grateful she could drown the noise of her own sobs in the thick squares of her grandmother's quilt.

Does everyone know?

Chichibow knew she was too old to still be unmarried. She knew by the gossipy women's silence when she sat amongst them that she had become a target of their talk.

Now she knew why.

My father wants to please Hadjo so he will marry me. Maybe he is here at my father's invitation.

Quiet sobs lifted and felled her chest. She covered her face with the quilt and sputtered aloud into the cloth.

"Thank you for coming." That is what my father said!

Drying her eyes and seeing clearly in her mind the conversation taking place only a few feet from her, Chichibow felt the strength of her resolve begin to grow. The faded colors of the quilt still held her grandmother's sweet and dusty scent. Chichibow wiped her cheeks and knotted the cloth in her palm, wishing she could sit at the old woman's feet and fall asleep to her soft humming.

"She will be home soon," she heard her father say.

Chichibow stiffened. If the men stayed in the room she was trapped and they would know she had been listening.

Unless I crawl out the window. Unless I go now. Why not go now?

———

Half an hour later Chichibow crouched in the cypress stumps behind Winnie's house, clutching a bundle of her belongings and watching for her friend.

"Winnie," she called out. "I need to talk to you."

"Is that you, Chichibow?" said Winnie's mother, stepping onto the back porch, lugging a heavy bucket. "Come on in the house, hon. Winnie's finishing the dishes."

"I'll just wait for her," said Chichibow. Winnie's mother shook her head and leaned her hip into the weight of the bucket as she made her way to the hog pen.

In a few minutes Winnie stuck her head out the door. "Don't be acting so funny, she said. "Come in the house and help me."

"No," Chichibow called in a loud whisper. "I am not coming inside." Soon Winnie joined her in the cypress stand, and her eyes fell to the bundle at Chichibow's side.

"You are doing it!" she said. "You are running away."

"I don't want to go by myself," said Chichibow. Winnie

opened her mouth to speak, but Chichibow held her hand up. "Think about what you say. I will understand. You don't have to say anything now."

"I want to talk about it now," said Winnie. "I have wanted to talk about it for a long time. I have known what would happen someday."

Chichibow's eyes filled with tears. "Do I want to hear this?" she asked.

"You need to hear this. The women gossip around here, you know."

Chichibow hung her head and closed her eyes, letting the tears flow down her cheeks. "How bad is the talk?"

"Bad enough," said Winnie. "Bad enough for me to know I never want to end up mean and gossipy like them. I am ready to go."

"Are you sure?" asked Chichibow.

"Yes."

"We have to go tonight. Hadjo is at my house now, wondering where I am. I saw his gray horse coming and hid in the house to listen to him and my father."

"What did they say?" asked Winnie.

"I couldn't stay. I couldn't bear to listen. My father acted like his servant, jumping around trying to please him. I got my things together and crawled out the window."

"I'll guess I'll have to do the same thing," said Winnie. "Sounds like we don't have much time."

————

Winnie left her parents with a lie that she knew she would regret for the rest of her life. "I won't be far off. We're just gonna talk, Chichibow and me."

"About what?" asked her mother.

"About some problems Chichibow's having."

"Don't you get involved, you hear me?"

"We are only talking. She is my friend."

An hour later Winnie and Chichibow crossed the Chattahoochee River. Stepping on the far shore and paying the ferryman with all the money they had, the girls realized they were truly on their own. The trip through Alabama was easier than they anticipated, as they soon joined with a cluster of Creek families on their way to Indian Territory. Seeking nothing but a spot by the evening fire after the long day's walk, the girls were welcomed by the travelers.

They were, for the trip at least, adopted by a large family with eight children and an old man who spent most of the day in the wagon, joining the girls only briefly each afternoon for the simple joy of walking. The girls cooked and helped with the little ones and could be counted on to tend to a sick child, gather firewood, or perform whatever task was needed, as eager to help as if they were family.

Only once did Chichibow fear that her whereabouts were known to her enemy. As the Creeks skirted Baton Rouge and prepared their camp before crossing the Mississippi River, a stranger appeared. His dark hat was pulled low over his eyes and he stood in the shadows on the fire's edge for almost an hour, till Chichibow was convinced she was the only one who could see him.

"Winnie?" she whispered.

"Yes?"

"Do you see that man?"

"Yes, I have kept my eye on him."

"What do you think he wants? Why doesn't he come into the light?" Winnie did not answer, but when she moved her blanket closer to the fire, Chichibow followed.

Soon they heard the sharp call of an owl in flight, and looking to the spot where the man had been standing, they saw no one. Winnie and Chichibow pulled their blankets tight over their heads and slipped into the cold escape of sleep.

The next morning the old man crawled from the wagon, saying, "Why don't I make myself useful and help you ladies with the firewood?"

"You don't have to do that," said Chichibow.

"No, I don't have to, but maybe you two should think about staying close to camp," said the old man.

Chichibow met Winnie's look, and the girls knew the reason the stranger had decided against entering the camp. The old man had powers the girls had not expected, and he was their friend. They smiled, and the old man was pleased at both their keen awareness and their silence.

"You two will be fine," he said.

———

Though the old man seldom left the wagon for the remainder of the trip, Chichibow and Winnie began calling him Grandfather and flung the full gale of their affections in his direction. They brought him berries and grapes they found by the roadside. They tossed long spiny flowers on him while he slept in the wagon bed in the afternoon, giggling when he sputtered awake. When he did choose to walk with the girls, they each held an arm to ease his descent from the wagon.

One day, as Chichibow walked beside him and Winnie was keeping the youngest together in the front of the wagon, Grandfather said, "You should not blame your father, you know."

"What do you mean?" she asked.

"Your father is a good man," he said. "He did the best he could with what he knew."

Chichibow thought for several minutes before replying.

"Does he miss me?"

"He does, and so does your mother."

"Should I go back?"

"You are doing the right thing to get as far away as you can."

"Can I ever be safe?" Chichibow asked.

"Not gonna be easy. I won't lie to you."

―――

When the Creeks arrived in Indian Territory, they moved to their allotted land and set about the task of clearing land and building. Chichibow and Winnie spoke of moving on, and the mother of the children, the missus, said, "If you want to stay, we can build you a small room away from the house."

The first several weeks passed by in a flurry of blister-raising hard work. Chichibow and Winnie rose in the crisp and cold of the morning and spent the day with the men, clearing pines and brush and driving away copperheads and rattlesnakes.

In the late afternoon, while the men soaked their feet in the cold spring water and fished, Chichibow and Winnie joined the women for cooking and scrubbing. The monotony was broken only by the necessary scolding and scrubbing of the always-underfoot children.

After ten days the girls had firm muscles on their arms and the strong gaze of hardened practicality on their faces. Though the men built a lean-to for the girls, Winnie and Chichibow continued to sleep under the nighttime summer sky.

One night the missus awakened the two, saying, "Can you come to the house? The old man is sick. He is asking for you both."

As they approached the larger house, Chichibow had an eerie feeling.

"Winnie," she said. "What if Grandfather dies?"

"I don't want to think about that," said Winnie.

When they entered his room, the old man motioned for them to kneel by his bed.

"I saw a man on horseback today," he said. "He was riding in the woods behind the house. He rode a gray horse, one I haven't seen before."

Chichibow closed her eyes and shivered.

"It was him," she said, so softly only the old man and Winnie heard her.

"Reach under my pillow."

Chichibow did as she was told and found a lone owl feather.

"Keep it with you at all times. You will not have long to wait."

———

The next evening, after a supper of corn soup and fried deer, Chichibow sat in the shade of a red oak tree. Leaning against the rough bark, she let her eyes follow the low-slung branch that stretched almost forty feet, barely touching their lean-to shack. She brushed the feather against her cheek and drifted to daydream thoughts of her family, her father's quiet manners and kindly ways and her mother's gritty spunk.

She did not notice when one of the children crept up behind her.

"Can I see?" the girl shouted, grabbing for the feather.

Chichibow jumped, startled, and whirled about.

"Boogabear!" she said. "Don't sneak up on me like that." Boogabear giggled and dove at Chichibow, burying her beaming face in her lap.

"You silly girl. What do you want?" Discreetly sliding the feather into the leaves at the base of the tree, Chichibow pressed her thumbs and forefingers into Boogabear's sides, like tiny, tickling bird claws.

As Boogabear laughed and struggled to free herself, Chichibow grabbed her from behind, wrapping her arm around her waist and pulling the wiggling child to her. Boogabear lifted her legs and twisted, flinging herself forward and lunging for the ground.

Somewhere in the free-flight fall and loss of balance, as the child's weight carried both of them—Chichibow and her prey—to the ground, wiggling turned to writhing and the child's struggle to free herself became urgent and real.

Chichibow saw the scene as if from above, the child slapping and biting the arms of her assailant, the cold expression of the man who dug his fingers into the child's ribs.

She heard the child cry.

She watched as the dark and powerful fingers curved, pulsing like bird claws grasping wood, and the fingernails lengthened to form a perfect point of sharpness, tearing through the cloth as brown and golden wings engulfed the now screaming child, smothering her with blanket completeness.

"*Cheeee cheeee! Cheeeecheeeebow!*"

Chichibow covered her ears to still the piercing screams. Boogabear rolled away, struggled to her feet, and ran crying to her house, where her mother stood staring in wonder at Chichibow.

"Chichibow?" said Winnie, emerging from the lean-to and placing a soft hand on her friend's shoulder. "Couldn't you see you were hurting her?"

Chichibow looked at Winnie with the desperate eyes of a lost child.

"Come with me," Winnie said, lifting Chichibow and helping her to the warm invisibility of the lean-to. She boiled water and made tea from a thick sassafras root, lifting her hand to silence Chichibow till the sweet aroma surrounded the two with a soft purple glow.

"You gonna be okay?" Winnie asked after a long silence.

Chichibow nodded.

"Boogabear was scared. I've never seen her crying like that."

"Will she be afraid of me?"

"She'll get over it pretty quick," said Winnie. "She's a child. Just be your usual self and she'll be alright."

"Something bad happened. I was out of myself, looking through somebody else's eyes."

"Maybe you should stay inside tonight. I can tell Boogabear's mother you were used to playing rough with your brothers. You just got carried away, that's all."

"I don't have any brothers."

"They don't know that," said Winnie. Chichibow sighed and tightened her lips in a look that said she did not like having to lie. She took a slow sip of tea and set the cup aside.

"It was him," she finally said.

"I know," said Winnie. "Don't talk about it. Just get well."

Chichibow turned to her corner and pulled a blanket over herself. As soon as she heard her friend's soft sleeping noises, Winnie went to the old man's bedside.

———

"Did you see him?" he asked.

"No," said Winnie. "I just saw the way Chichibow grabbed at her. It was not Chichibow."

"No," the old man said. "It was not Chichibow. He is close, even now. He knows I am sick, and he is hanging around till I can't help you anymore."

"What can we do?"

"Sleep inside. Stay close to each other. Maybe put something in front of the door so you know if anybody comes in."

The old man took a deep breath and looked to the ceiling. He closed his eyelids only halfway and his head lolled back on the pillow, rolling almost imperceptively from side to side. His eyelids fluttered.

Winnie knew he was seeing Hadjo come for Chichibow. He lifted his hand from his side and held it still, pointing to the ceiling, for almost a minute. He took another long breath and slowly curled and uncurled his fingers, calling Winnie closer. She leaned to hear him.

"The feather," he said in a hoarse whisper, barely moving his lips. "Where is the owl feather?" Winnie backed away.

"I don't know," she said, and the old man opened his eyes as if awakening from a dream.

"You should maybe go now." The missus stood dark and silhouetted in the doorway. "He is tired. He needs his rest."

Winnie averted her eyes and quickly left the house. While Chichibow slept, she scoured the lean-to looking for the owl feather, unrolling bundles and digging into bags, both her own and Chichibow's. She retraced their path to the lean-to, approaching and circling the tree several times, in case the feather had fallen from Chichibow's pocket.

The feather slipped still deeper beneath the leaves, waiting for the child.

———

"I had a good sleep. I needed it," Chichibow said. She and Winnie sat like friendly watchdogs on either side of the narrow door to the lean-to, staring at the flickering stars. The sky was clear and shone bright blue with only a sliver of moon.

"I wonder if my father is looking at the same sky, wondering where I am. He likes to sit in his chair on the back porch and just stare at the night sky."

"Same with mine," said Winnie. "I'll make us some more tea." She stood to go, and Chichibow touched her skirt as she passed through the doorway.

"I am going to miss you," Chichibow said.

"I will only be gone for a few minutes," said Winnie, and the two friends smiled at Winnie's humor, knowing as only friends can their impending separation.

Chichibow closed her eyes and felt the wetness behind her eyelids. *I will truly miss you, my deepest, dearest friend,* she thought.

———

Though she was relieved, Chichibow at first protested

when Winnie insisted they sleep inside. Winnie spread her sleeping blanket near the doorway, clutching the knife she used for gutting deer, and Chichibow bedded down by the far wall.

When the soft scratching came, Chichibow was unafraid. She had waited so long for this, she only hoped that whatever happened would happen quickly. She touched the skinny cane poles of the wall and felt their vibration.

He is right beside me, on the other side of this wall, she thought. She lay still, and in the dim light watched a powerful claw pricking its way between two brittle poles.

"Chichibow," Winnie whispered. "You have to move. Roll away from the wall slowly. Do it now."

With the splintery opening several inches wide, the owl stretched his claw far into the lean-to, only inches from Chichibow's face.

"Chichibow!" Winnie shouted.

Chichibow flung her head back as sharp claws came at her. She leapt to her feet and Winnie pulled her to the back of the lean-to. The owl continued scratching and widening the gap, filling the room with an eerie gnawing sound.

When the hole was the size of a large man's fist, he suddenly withdrew his claw. For half a minute the girls heard only the sound of their own breathing. Then a ball of feathers thrust into view and they realized they were looking at the owl's head as he struggled to squeeze his entire body through the opening.

"Come on," Chichibow whispered. "You can do it."

"Chichibow, what is happening?"

"You know what is happening," she said. "He is here," and as if in response to her words, the owl eased himself through the hole and stepped to the floor.

A tremor shook every feather on the bird. He twirled and turned, stomping his claws and whirling in an ugly jerking dance. The girls clung to each other as the owl grew larger with every revolution, lifting first one wing and then the other, till Chichibow and Winnie felt limp from the tension of watching.

Almost without their noticing, the owl stopped his dancing and Hadjo stood before them.

Without hesitating, he lunged at Chichibow, clutched her arm, and spun her to the ground. Chichibow waved her free fist at him, and Hadjo responded by twisting her arm behind her back as she struggled to strike him with her other hand.

Suddenly a small shadow appeared in the doorway, followed by a child's voice.

"Chichibow?" Hadjo and the girls turned to see Boogabear walking across the room.

"Grandfather told me to bring this to you," she said, reaching behind her back and handing Chichibow the feather. In the quick moment of confusion, Winnie dove for her knife and thrust it beneath Chichibow's arms and into Hadjo's ribcage.

Hadjo grimaced at the child, relaxing his grip as his hand clutched at the knife. Chichibow wrenched her arm free and brushed the owl feather across his face. With the touch of the feather, Hadjo shuddered and his body went into a series of spasms. A minute later he lay dead at their feet.

Winnie held Chichibow close, pulling her face to her shoulder. She took a deep breath and smoothed Chichibow's hair to ease her sobbing. After a long, sweet moment, Chichibow wiped her eyes.

"Thank you," she said, and her mouth quivered in the beginning of a smile. Winnie met her eyes and nodded.

"I always believe in you, even when you lose sight of your own strength," she said. "I am your friend, good Chichibow."

"I'm your friend, too," said Boogabear, and Chichibow stooped and lifted the child into her arms.

Corn Lady

The Billie family lived on the edge of the forest where the game ran plentiful and the rains kept the crops in abundance. They knew of the dangers to the north, so they kept quietly to themselves, enjoying their children and friends. Some might say they were poor, living as they did in small chickees—huts of palm roofs supported by cypress pillars with no walls—but they were as rich as they knew how to be.

The men sometimes disappeared in the forest for days in search of deer and other large game. The women tended the gardens while the children swam in the nearby ponds and played in the woods on the fringe of town.

One day the older children left the infant Tom Billie, wrapped in a thin blanket and leaning against the pole of a chickee, while they ran to the woods following the sound of a strange bird. Someone later said it was an owl, but others thought that was only to explain the death of Tom Billie, for the call of an owl *can* mean death.

When the children returned, having found no strange bird, they also found no Tom Billie. His mother and sisters cried out and called for him, beating the bushes and underbrush with cane poles for any sign of Tom, but he seemed to have vanished from the face of the earth.

"You cannot blame the children," said Tom Billie's mother, when the men returned from hunting. "The chickee should be safe. They did not go far."

Tom's father called a medicine man, an older Seminole who lived deep in the woods, and that evening everyone from the small village came to listen to the old man.

"Many unusual things live in the swamps," he said. "There are Little People, as you know. They are medicine people who teach those of us who hear the secrets of their ways. They will sometimes steal children for a few days and begin their instruction. In this way they mark those who will later be healing people, doctors." Seeing hope in the eyes of Tom Billie's parents, the medicine man continued.

"I do not think that is what has happened to this little one. Unseen ones, invisible ones, also live in the swamps. They carry off children, as well. I think that is what happened to Tom Billie."

"How long do the unseen ones keep a child before they return him?" asked Tom's mother.

The medicine man looked at Tom's father, hung his head, and said, "I think your child is still alive, somewhere in the swamps. But it is unlikely you will ever see him again. The unseen ones will never return him, and looking for them will not bring back your child." He rose and left Tom Billie's family to deal with the loss of their brother and son.

Years went by, and the boy's family finally gave up all hope of finding the boy. With the passage of time, Tom Billie was no longer part of their lives.

As the medicine man had said, Tom Billie was still alive, living with a woman, a witch, who loved him dearly. They lived on an island deep in the swamp, just the two of them, in a homestead of three chickees—one for eating, one for sleeping, and one used only for cooking. The witch was hideously ugly, but with no other people about, the boy saw only a kindly mother, not an ugly witch ashamed of her appearance.

The woman realized that when the boy grew older he would discover the truth about himself. She knew he would leave her to find his own family, so she loved him and cared for him as if every day with him might be the last. Her greatest dread was the moment when he would see other people and realize how ugly she was. As he grew to be a teenager, she knew the time for his departure was nearing.

"Why don't I go into the swamp and find meat to put in the sofkee*?" he asked one evening, as she stirred the corn soup.

"You do not know the woods," she said. "You might get lost, and I am too old to find my lost boy."

"I will never know the woods from under the roof of this chickee," he said. Seeing the pain in her eyes, he quickly added, "You are right. Sofkee doesn't need meat." The old woman lifted her head and glanced at the boy beneath heavy eyelids, and he smiled and touched her hand.

I am beautiful in his unknowing eyes," she thought. *"Maybe I can always be.*

The boy, Tom Billie, fell asleep that evening with questions swirling in his mind. *We have no garden, but she always has corn for sofkee. What is she hiding from me?*

The next morning he only pretended to be asleep when she arose for her usual morning walk, from which she always returned with a basket of corn. He followed her to a clear water stream and watched, unseen, from the palmetto bushes on the shore. The old woman waded into the stream and dipped her hands in the water, swirling small circles on the surface. She cupped water in her hands and leaned her head back as the cooling water fell across her face.

This is a time of great happiness for her, thought Tom Billie, and at that moment he realized he cared deeply for this old woman.

She knelt in the stream and scrubbed her ankles and legs with moss hanging from the cypress trees. Tom Billie settled

---

*A traditional dish usually served at Creek and Seminole gatherings, sofkee is boiled corn sweetened with sugar and served in a cup

in the bushes, hiding and waiting for her to pass him on her way to the chickees, when he saw something he could not believe was happening.

The old woman sat on a stump and began rubbing her legs over the basket. Corn kernels fell from her legs, filling the basket.

This is where the corn comes from! he thought. He ran quickly to his bed and pretended to be asleep when she returned. She parched the corn, pounded it into cornmeal, and cooked the sofkee over the open fire.

When he did not roll over and awaken with the noise of the pounding, she said, "You can get up, now. I know you followed me. You know about me, and it is alright. You had to know someday.

"I have pretended you were my son. I am ugly. I am a witch, and no one would ever even look at me. I knew I would never have children of my own."

"Where did I come from?" asked Tom Billie.

"You come from several days to the east, across the swamp river and toward the rising sun. Your family name is Billie. You have sisters and brothers and anyone can direct you to your people." She went to the sleeping chickee and returned carrying a necklace. "You were wearing this when I took you. Your family will know you when they see the necklace."

"I do not know what to do," said Tom Billie.

"The first thing you must do is forget about this old woman. Forget about me. I have been blessed to have you as my son for all these years. Try to forgive my taking you."

"You have taken care of me. Why should I forgive you?" asked Tom.

"I hope you always feel that way," the old woman said. She took Tom Billie by both hands and moved his palms to her cheeks. He felt her warm tears as she brushed her face against his skin for the final time.

After a long moment, the woman dried her cheeks with her skirt and said, "I will leave a small fire burning overnight. You must arise after midnight and gather everything you can carry. Remember, you have a long trip ahead of you, so travel light.

"Just before you go, take three sticks from the fire and toss them on the dried roofs of the chickees. Do not leave until you are certain all of the chickees are burning. Then run as if your life depended on it. Run to your family."

"I cannot leave you here," said Tom Billie.

"You will think differently in the morning," she said.

That night, just after midnight, Tom arose and gathered his bundle of clothes. He smelled the cypress wood burning and quietly approached the fire. Only then did he truly realize what the old woman was asking him to do.

With tears streaming down his face, he took a stick from the fire and threw it onto the first chickee, the sleeping chickee. He saw the dried leaves bursting into flames and imagined the old woman curling under her blanket till the flames found her. He dashed beneath the falling, crackling flames to the witch's bed, intending to drag her to safety. The bed was empty.

She is safe. She has gone to the woods, he thought.

From a dark corner of the cooking chickee, the old woman watched and smiled a proud and wistful smile, seeing the boy's efforts to save her. By the time the flames wrapped themselves around her, Tom Billie was on the shore and running full speed to the eastern sunrise.

Two days later he entered a clearing with dozens of chickees. He moved in a slow pace, circling the edge of the woods so as not to frighten the people who lived there.

"Who are you?" a young man asked, stepping from the shadows of a chickee.

"My family name is Billie."

"Where do you come from?"

"I think I was born here, years ago," said Tom. "Do the Billies live here?"

"Yes," said the young man. "But I do not remember you." An older man sitting in a nearby doorway heard the two talking and said, "There was a baby stolen from the Billies a long time ago."

He led Tom to a chickee where an old woman sat in the shade, repairing a torn shirt. As soon as she looked into his eyes, the woman stood and dropped the shirt to the ground.

"Tom? Tom Billie? You are my son," she said, running to him and throwing her arms around him. Soon everyone in the village knew of the return of Tom Billie.

After several days of celebrating and telling his family of the kindly woman who took care of him all those years, Tom said, "I would like to take you all to the chickee and see where I lived."

The next morning, several men rose before sunrise and accompanied Tom on the trip into the western swamps.

Hoping that Tom's memories of her would be happy ones, the old woman had prepared a gift for him and his people, should they seek her home in peace. As they topped the final hill overlooking the island in the swamp, the men beheld a glorious sight that would change the lives of all Seminole people from that day forward.

Where once stood three chickees, now waved hundreds of cornstalks, dancing in the breeze of the old woman's spirit.

As she hovered over the scene of men gathering seed and filling their baskets with sweet yellow corn, the old woman smiled in the knowledge that she would forever be beautiful in the eyes of young Tom Billie.